BUG HUNT

GAYNE C. YOUNG

SEVERED PRESS
HOBART TASMANIA

BUG HUNT

Copyright © 2018 Gayne C. Young
Copyright © 2018 by Severed Press

WWW.SEVEREDPRESS.COM

ISBN: *978-1-925840-18-6*

For Allison and Barrett

1.

"SHOOT! Shoot now, Goddammit!"

Joel Andrews stood motionless, a victim of his own panic. Blood drained from his face, his legs turned to jelly, his hands palsied.

Over 5,000 pounds of armored steel steamrolled toward him. The ground trembled, huge clouds of dust burst upward. The juggernaut slammed into Joel. The force of such enormity propelled forward at 30 miles per hour shot his head back and snapped his vertebrae. His body fell limp, paralyzation replacing the panic that kept him from controlling his body. The monstrosity's goliath mandibles squeezed Joel's chest with the force of a hydraulic press.

Joel screamed.

Bones snapped.

Air escaped his lungs in a harrowing gasp.

Thunder clapped as Burke Tyler fired his .600 N.E. from 15 yards away. The 900-grain bullet punched through chitin armor with a piercing scream. Hemolymph exploded outward in arterial spray. Burke fired once more, driving a hole into the beast's head only five inches from the first. Burke's Heym double rifle broke.

Shells ejected.

Burke dropped two in the tubes, snapped the barrels shut, aimed, and fired once more.

The ant crashed forward and onto the ground with an explosion of dirt and vegetation. Its mandibles cinched completely closed and Joel's body was halved. Blood and intestinal fluids, viscera and other bodily liquids pooled in the dirt below his broken body. Burke climbed upon the fallen insect's body and fired once more into its primitive brain.

"Goddammit," he barked. "God damn it all."

2.

"Crushed his ribs. Shattered 'em so badly the bones fused into his vertebrae. All in less than a second."

"Not much of a sales pitch."

"I'm not here to sell you. That's been done. I'm here to warn you…"

"Warn me?!"

Burke could already tell he didn't like the client. He was arrogant. Too cocksure for his own good. One of those entitled rich pricks that felt he had to monopolize the conversation because he knew more than the person leading it. Not only were assholes like this a pain in the ass to have on a safari, but they could be dangerous as well. They could miss shots. Fail to drop an animal or panic in the face of a charge. An example being the hunter he'd just detailed, the one that came back with a far more interesting vertebra than the one he had left with.

"Warn you of the dangers. To be honest with you," Burke continued, trying not to let his opinion of Champe Carter influence the tone of his voice.

"I can appreciate that," Champe interrupted once more. "Please do."

"Regardless of the bugs you choose to hunt," Burke began again, "poor judgment or hesitation on any part can and will be lethal. As I've said, these things are far more dangerous than anything else you can hunt on Earth, legal or illegal."

Champe's face lit up in excitement. This is what he wanted to hear. What he wanted to experience. He wanted to test himself, test himself in a setting built around life and death. Where a certain outcome couldn't be bought and life wasn't guaranteed. Champe's boss David Braxton had told Champe that three clients had died in the last two years on safaris with MicroTech. Only David's wealth and a whole lot of legal wrangling had kept the clients' deaths from becoming public. Not that MicroTech or the safaris were public to begin with. Very few could afford the hunts MicroTech offered and even fewer had actually heard of the company or of the technology that made it possible.

"I'm well aware of the risks," Champe proudly stated. "And of what the animals can do. How do I prove that to you?"

"Practicing for what's to come is a poor substitute to actually experiencing it first hand," Burke explained. "But we have a live fire cinema projection range facility on campus—"

"I've been to one of those," Champe once again interrupted. "Hell'uva lotta fun. Ya shoot at game animals projected life-size on a movie screen."

Burke nodded.

"Ours uses footage from actual safaris we've conducted. It'll show the bugs' full size. I've penciled us in for tomorrow morning. Nine work?"

"I'll make it work."

"What do you plan on shooting?"

"I've got a Kreighoff double .500 Nitro Express. It's a freakin' hammer."

"You've shot it before?"

"Oh hell yeah," Champe scoffed. "Who'd plan a safari like this without practicing for months ahead of time?"

"You'd be surprised," Burke assured him. "Very surprised."

3.

Burke entered his apartment and immediately grabbed a beer from the fridge. He took a long pull from the bottle then undressed and entered the shower with beer in hand. By the time he exited the bath, he had finished the beer. He put on a pair of ratty khaki shorts and a worn chambray shirt, grabbed another beer, and headed to the porch. He lit a cigar and sat back in his recliner and gazed upon the few pecan trees in the quad below.

The campus was small as tech campuses went. At only five acres, it consisted of a small parking lot, a small office building, a three-story lab, and a few outbuildings. His apartment was located in one of these outlying buildings. The first floor was a garage that was used mainly as storage while the second floor had been converted into an efficiency apartment by the earlier owners. Burke hated the apartment. Hated the campus and most of the people he dealt with during the day. He didn't understand what most of the techs he interacted with actually did for a living nor did he care. All he cared about was having a job and the one he had with MicroTech was about the only one for a man of his skills left in the world.

It had been a long road from his youth in Meridian, Texas to living on a tech campus outside of Austin and guiding for what he called bug hunts. At 17 years old, Burke quit high school, put his abusive upbringing in the rear mirror, and headed out into the world to claim what was his. A stint in the Army gave him a taste for travel and adventure and taught him how to hold his own under pressure. Afterward, he worked private security for a wealthy businessman by the name of John Gates that introduced him to the thrill of big game hunting when Burke accompanied him to Botswana for an elephant hunt. Burke fell in love with the country and of time spent afield. When he told his boss at the end of the hunt he was thinking of staying on the continent, Mr. Gates offered Burke a deal he couldn't pass up.

Burke was to earn his Professional Hunting license in South Africa under the tutelage of Melcom Els. In addition, Melcom would teach him all that he could about the safari business and game management. When Melcom felt he was ready, Burke would take over the hunting operation that he had just sold to Mr. Gates.

For the next 15 years, Burke guided clients after leopard, lion, buffalo, elephant, rhino, and plains game. He continued doing so after Mr. Gates died and left him the business and up until big game hunting was banned on most of the continent. Burke retired back in Texas content to live out the rest of his life, slowly drinking himself to death on the shores of Lake Amistad, when he was approached about guiding hunters once more, this time on a 20,000-acre game ranch near Uvalde. Burke guided hunters after antelope imported from Africa and Asia and deer from Europe. He told clients stories from his days of hunting Africa and feigned interest in their stories about how wealthy they were and how they got that way.

One client, David Braxton, was different. Rather than bore Burke with stories that tried to top his own, David talked about the future. One of his companies—of which he owned many—had invented a technology that could shrink the distance between molecules. Not only did the process have almost unlimited industrial applications but could also provide David access to a new frontier, one completely virgin and completely unknown.

Burke listened intently to David's dreams and by the end of the long weekend agreed to hire on as his Professional Hunter. In the four years since, Burke had guided David on over 30 safaris. David had opened the hunts to a few select friends and associates who had money to spend on such extravagances two years ago. The hunts were secret, as the government had yet to approve the shrink technology for use of any kind, a situation that millions upon millions of dollars paid to the right politicians would surely rectify soon.

Burke killed his beer and walked inside to get another. He had a bottle in his hand then changed his mind and poured a tall glass of Patrón Silver tequila instead. He retreated back to the porch and took his place in the recliner.

4.

Champe rolled off of Scarlett and worked to catch his breath. Scarlett rolled in the opposite direction and out of bed with boundless energy. She stretched to the heavens then almost skipped to Champe's side of the bed and began jerking his hand.

"Come on!" she toyed. "Let's swim. You got me all sweaty."

"Gimme a sec."

"No way. Let's go." Scarlett leaned over and kissed Champe then slapped his chest. "Come on. I'll grab some drinks. Meet you out there."

He watched her bound out of his bedroom and toward the kitchen. He stood and made his way to the French doors that opened out to his back deck and the pool beyond it. The night air was humid for August and Austin's city lights bathed his backyard in electric shades of blue. He dove into the pool, swam its distance underwater, and surfaced to see Scarlett walking toward him. He watched her naked form approach and marveled at her body. Youth and genetics had given her a great start; plastic surgery and her husband's money spent on day after day at the spa made her unbelievable.

Scarlett kneeled next to him, placed two bottles of Sol beer on the side of the pool then eased into the water. She floated over to Champe, kissed him deeply, handed him one of the beers, then took the other into her hand. They toasted then drank.

"So," Scarlett began, her eyes dancing in excitement, "did you tell him I'm coming on the hunt?"

"Not yet."

Scarlett playful slapped Champe's shoulder then took a long pull on her beer.

"I'm meeting up with him tomorrow," Champe explained. "We're gonna run through some simulations at the range. Imagine we'll make final arrangements for the hunt after that. I'll tell him then."

Scarlett smiled and leaned in to kiss Champe once more.

"You sure no one knows you down at MicroTech?" Champe asked. "You've never met Burke Tyler?"

"We don't run in the same circles," Scarlett laughed.

"He's your husband's right-hand man."

"David has lots of right-hand men. None of which know me or would go to him with anything bad about me. They're all scared of him. Scared of what he can do and have done…"

Champe shook his hands and eerily booed as if he was a ghost or haunting spirit.

"I know you're not scared of him," Scarlett said, laughing.

"A little bit," Champe admitted, holding his fingers a few millimeters apart to indicate how little a bit was.

"You don't act like you're scared of getting caught when we're in there," Scarlett cooed, tilting her head in the direction of Champe's bedroom. "Or all the other places you do me."

"Do you!" Champe laughed.

"Yeah!" Scarlett cackled. "Do me good!"

Scarlett took another drink and Champe followed suit.

"And, this weekend, you'll do me when I'm smaller than an ant!"

5.

"If you've done this before, then you know the drill," Burke explained. "Each shot you fire into the screen will pause the film. A red dot will appear where the bullet struck."

Champe nodded then looked from Burke to the dark two-story cinema screen before him.

"Let's look at some pics before we start," Burke said.

He pressed a sequence of keys on the iPad he held and the screen illuminated.

"Holy shit," Champe gasped, watching the image of a bullet ant materialize on the screen. "Is that how big he'll be?"

"Our size is up to you," Burke explained. "But the scale you're looking at is what I recommend..." "Then let's do that," Champe interrupted, staring in awe at the monster before him.

"That'll make him seven foot at the shoulder," Burke began again. "Rhino size. Close to five, five and a half thousand pounds..."

"How fast?"

"Too fast. You don't want him charging. We've clocked one at 35 miles per hour."

"Holy shit."

"Holy shit is right."

Burke pressed another button on his iPad and a red target appeared on the screen. Burke moved the target with his finger on the tablet until it sat at the top of the ant's head.

"Here's where ya wanna hit him," Burke instructed. "Brain pan. The exoskeleton is made of chitin. It's concrete tough. Takes a hell'uva punch to get through."

Champe smiled and held aloft his .500 N.E.

"That'll do it, if you hit him right. Brain's as primitive as they come. But destroy the brain and he will fall."

Burke moved the red target to the ant's back.

"Heart's actually a long tube that runs the length of his back. Brain's your first choice. Heart's the second."

Burke dropped the target to just below the heart.

"And this is the nerve cord. Knock this out n' he won't go far."

"Brain first," Champe repeated as if making a list in his mind.

"I'll tell you where to shoot if and when a shot presents itself," Burke assured. "I'm just showing you the basics."

Champe nodded.

"You ready to try some shooting?"

Champe nodded and smiled. He held his rifle across his chest and exclaimed, "Hell yeah."

Burke worked the tablet and the screen flickered. The scene that came to light was of a thick forest.

"Is that…grass?" Champe asked.

"Yep. You're in the tall grass…"

"Looks like cactus trees or something," Champe said, pointing at what appeared to be green tree trucks covered in sharpened horns.

"And those spikes are every bit as sharp as cactus thorns."

Champe stared in disbelief at the alien world presented on the screen before him. His palms started to sweat and his body beamed in excitement. This was everything he wanted and more so. He was ready for the adventure of his life.

"The camera's gonna pan as if we're walking through the grasses," Burke explained, gesturing to the screen before them. "At some point, we'll run into the same species of—"

"*Paraponera clavata*," Champe almost sang. "The bullet ant."

"If you say so," Burke almost laughed. "I'm not required to know their Latin names. When we see one, wait for me to give the command to shoot."

Champe nodded in agreement, a smile plastered on his face.

"When I say 'shoot,' I want you to hit your target twice then reload as fast as you can."

Champe nodded again then took two cigar-sized .500 bullets from his ammo belt and placed them between the fingers of his left hand. He held his rifle, barrel down on the right side of his body then lifted it to across his chest with the barrel pointing outward from his left shoulder. Burke pressed a command on his iPad and the film began. Champe was the very picture of bliss.

The two men "walked" through the alien landscape. The camera snaked through the forest at an easy pace and Champe's heart pounded with excitement. They came around a blade of grass to an opening bathed in light. Dark tubular spears pointed from the grasses on the right and Champe gripped his rifle tighter.

"Antenna," Champe whispered.

Burke nodded in agreement then halfway smiled at the fact that Champe had whispered just as he should in the field. If he practiced like the real thing, then the real thing would be a whole lot better.

And far easier.

The antenna swayed gently back and forth some 10 to 15 feet off the ground. Champe was so fixated on them that he failed to see the heavy mandibles several feet below them exit the forest. These were followed by the front of the head. Champe panned down to see the ant's massive head come fully into view. He instinctively situated his rifle into position and held it tight against his shoulder.

"Hold," Burke whispered. "Hang tight."

"What's the distance? How far away is he?" Champe whispered in response.

"Too far. Hundred fifty yards…"

"I can hit him at that distance."

"Don't care." Burke's whisper increased in pitch. "Not a risk we need to take with open sights."

Champe nodded and stared at the large platter-sized eye on the game animal before him. It was the color of pitch and lifeless.

No pupil.

No reflection.

Just a black halved orb.

The ant's antennae swayed toward the two men. Its head pivoted and pointed in Champe's direction. The loud hiss of escaping steam echoed through the grasses as it opened its mandibles wide.

"Get ready," Burke warned.

"He's gonna charge," Champe mumbled to himself in excitement. The adrenaline in his body pooled in his chest as if ready to burst outward.

The hissing grew in volume and the ant bolted forward. Champe watched in disbelief. The speed of the beast was unreal. The ant barreled forward, its size increasing by the nanosecond.

Trees swayed. Dirt exploded beneath the animal's heavy-clawed feet. Champe held the rifle tight. His chest compressed and he forgot to breathe.

"Take him!" Burke said in a normal voice. "Two in the brain. Front on."

Champe pulled the first trigger and the right barrel of the Kreighoff boomed. The 570-grain bullet slammed into the ant's head at 2,150 feet per second, exploding a hole the size of a child's fist. The beast wobbled but continued forward. Champe eased the second trigger back and the left barrel thundered. Two empty shell casings launched upwards in a brass-colored blur and Champe swung his left hand over the two empty pipes and dropped in his second set of bullets. He closed the breach with a heavy flick and shouldered the rifle once more. He found the ant in his sights then realized the simulation had halted. The ant projected on screen stood lifeless.

"Safety on," Burke instructed.

Champe complied and dropped the rifle to his side.

"Let's see how you did." Burke swiped at his tablet as two red dots appeared on the ant's head not three inches apart.

Champe beamed from ear to ear.

"Damn good shooting," Burke complimented. "Really good. You dropped him there."

"How far?"

"That would have been 30 maybe 35 yards."

"Damn!"

"We don't want him any closer."

Champe continued beaming.

"Seriously though," Burke continued. "You did good. Real good."

Champe swung his rifle to his left side and held his right hand out to Burke. The men shook and Champe continued basking in his elation. Burke smiled slightly in return then said, "Calm it down. We're gonna try a few more."

6.

Champe took the table lighter from Burke and rolled the end of his cigar in the flame then put it in his mouth and finished the job of lighting it. He killed the flame on the lighter and placed it on the table. He raised his glass of Patrón Silver tequila and Burke matched him.

"Cheers," Champe offered.

"Cheers," Burke echoed.

They had spent most of the morning in the cinema practicing various scenarios and hunting different species. Champe had done well "killing" three bullet ants, a ghost ant, two species of rhinoceros beetle, and a walking stick.

"Give your shoulder some rest until Friday," Burke suggested. "I don't want you tensing up."

"Then we're on for Friday?" Champe almost exploded. "It's a go?"

Burke nodded and Champe slapped the table in excitement then laughed at the sound and looked around the patio to make sure he hadn't disturbed anyone. Noting that the courtyard of the tech campus was empty, he let out a fairly loud "whoop."

Burke tossed a legal pad on the table then took a sip from his drink.

"You're wanting the full ride?" Burke began. "Two nights. Three days?"

Champe puffed his cigar and nodded.

"I'll have the cook get with you concerning meals and beverage choice. I have a videographer. He's very good. Can put together a nice video after the hunt..."

"Tack that on. Sounds great."

"A word of warning. Be careful who you show it to. No social media. Of any kind. The technology we're using isn't exactly legal yet."

"I understand," Champe said, trying to blow a smoke ring.

"What species?" Burke began again. "And how many of each?"

Champe squinted in thought. He took another drink then asked, "What do you recommend? Number wise?"

"Depends on the species but two on Friday is fine if everything goes according to plan. Two or three Saturday. I'd like to pull out by mid-afternoon on Sunday so one's good. Maybe two."

"Sounds good," Champe agreed. "What do you recommend species wise? Ants were fun."

"We can do all ants. They're my favorite. Remind me of Cape buffalo hunting back in Africa. They make for a great hunt."

"I'd like to do something more than just ants," Champe confessed. "I mean hunting them today was a blast…"

"No," Burke interrupted. "Hunting them in the cinema is fun. Hunting them in real life is a blast."

Champe smiled. "I can't wait! Oh. How about a rhino beetle? Do you have praying mantis? That would be…"

"We can hunt almost anything but you'll have to do mantis on a return trip. I'll need to see you in the field before I'll guide you to one of those…"

"Why?"

"They're far too fast. They put cheetahs to shame. And just as dangerous."

"But you saw me today…"

"Do well on this hunt then we'll talk hunting mantis on a future hunt."

Champe reluctantly agreed and killed his drink. He stood and poured himself another tequila from the outside bar.

"Ice?" he asked, looking for a cooler or bucket.

Burke motioned to the cabinet to the left of the sink. Champe opened it and took a handful of cubes and dropped them in his glass. He took a sip and returned to his chair.

"I have lady companion that'll be coming with me," Champe began anew. "She'll just be an observer. She won't be hunting."

Burke tried to hide the scowl that he was developing. He didn't have anything against women on safari. He just had something against distractions on safari and distractions could be dangerous.

Very dangerous.

"She'll cost the same as you…"

"Agreed…"

"And she follows my instruction the same as you or she's out…"

"Agreed."

"I'm dead serious."

"I understand," Champe assured. "She won't be any trouble. No trouble. I promise."

7.

Maria Flores entered David Braxton's office and shut the door. She handed her employer a thick folder then sat in the chair opposite his desk. David began to open the folder then thought the better of it and instead gestured for Maria to begin.

"It's Champe Carter…"

"That son of a bitch," David exploded through clenched teeth. He paused in thought for a moment then nodded for Maria to continue.

"They've been seeing each other for at least three months."

"At least?"

"Maybe longer. I'm not sure. But fairly regularly for the past three months."

"Where?"

"They've been fairly discrete. Mostly getting together at his home. Two weekends away but during both they've kept their activities low key. Staying at lower end motels. Eating at chain restaurants. Paying with cash."

"How many people know about it?"

"No one in the public that I could ascertain. She has taken a few photos of the two of them, some of just him in various states of undress, with her phone but hasn't sent them to anyone."

David's jaw tightened further as betrayal and anger boiled beneath his skin. Her cheating was one thing, and given her young age, almost to be expected. Champe's involvement was another matter. He didn't have the excuse of immaturity. He knew what he was doing and it was deliberate.

"However, they do have plans to hunt with Burke this weekend," Maria continued.

"Does Burke know about them?"

"It's doubtful. Champe simply told Burke he was bringing a lady friend. Burke has never met your wife nor do I believe he knows what she looks like. He avoids social media and barely spends anytime online."

"Who else is going?" David asked. "The cook? Anyone else?"

"Yes, sir. Bert Mikosh will be serving as the cook. A videographer named Andrew Matthes will be filming the hunt. It's reasonable to assume that both are familiar with your wife given her highly visible media presence."

That highly visible media presence was the real issue, David thought.

News of his wife's infidelity—with one of his vice presidents no less—would undoubtedly harm his chances for having his MicroTech's shrink technology receive governmental approval. Not only that, but the scandal would undoubtedly harm his other companies' reputation and possibly result is losses of millions of dollars.

Then there was the cost of divorce. He'd already gone through that twice before and the financial ramifications were devastating. Even with a prenuptial agreement and the proof that Maria had obtained of Scarlett's repeated infidelity, Scarlett would still take him to the cleaners.

No.

It was better to cut his losses ahead of time. There was simply too much at stake not to do so. He hated the idea of losing Burke but another Professional Hunter could be found. One that wouldn't have the opportunity to tell the world how his wife spent a romantic weekend away with one of his vice presidents.

Damn that Champe Carter.

What a son of a bitch.

David sat for a moment longer then slid the folder across his desk in Maria's direction. Maria stood and took the folder.

"You'll make sure all of this is taken care of?"

"Yes, sir. It will be dealt with accordingly."

8.

"Alex. Alex Clayton."

Burke stood in the doorway of his apartment looking at the man whose name was apparently Alex Clayton.

"Yeah..."

The man named Alex Clayton continued standing in the doorway, a blank stare on his face.

"And? What do you want?" Burke continued.

Alex stood in momentary paralysis. He stared at Burke in disbelief. How could this guy not recognize him?

"I've shrunk you maybe two hundred times..."

"Oh yeah," Burke said, finally registering who this guy was. He looked different out of his white lab coat. "Come in. Whatcha need?"

"No, I've gotta get," Alex said nervously. He stood motionless in the doorway. "I just wanted to let you know I won't be there tomorrow so Eric will be putting you into the field by himself."

"Can he do it by himself?" Burke asked.

"Oh yeah," Alex enthusiastically replied. "The whole thing's nearly automated as it is. We just like to have two operators. Ya know. Just in case."

"You're the scientists. If you say it's fine, then I guess it's fine."

"It'll be fine." Alex smiled. "And even if it isn't, Eric knows how to get a hold of me."

"Going someplace fun then?"

"Huh? Oh, no. I'll be at home. Human Resources called. Well, MicroTech doesn't have an HR department I don't think. Human

Resources from our parent company called. Elizabeth something. She told me I'd worked too many weekends or something and not to come in."

Burke took a drink from his tequila and huffed, "That was far more info than I needed, kid."

Alex laughed. "Yeah. I guess I went on there for a bit. But just wanted to let you know that I won't be there."

Burke said, "Got it," shut the door, and went to top off his drink.

9.

Burke met Champe and Scarlett in the parking lot outside the main building of the tech campus. Champe was dressed in well-worn hunting attire while Scarlett's form-fitting shorts and cleavage-enhancing shirt all but had the price tags still on them. She'd apparently done some shopping in anticipation of her weekend away. A lot of shopping given the amount of luggage she was bringing with her.

Champe introduced Burke to Scarlett by her first name only then helped Burke to load their luggage onto a flat cart. The three entered the building then made their way to a large lab where they were met by Eric. Introductions were made and both Champe's and Scarlett's excitement levels increased intensely.

"Is this it?" Champe almost exploded pointing to what appeared to be a large terrarium sitting on a table on the far side of the lab behind surgical-grade plastic sheeting.

Burke moved before Champe to make sure he didn't walk closer to the sealed environment.

"Yes," Eric quickly answered. "But let's stay on this side of the room for now. The area is climate controlled and sealed off in order to ensure the integrity of the environment."

"Go ahead and give them the rundown," Burke interrupted.

Eric put his hands into his white lab coat and began.

"When you're ready, you and your luggage will enter this chamber," Eric said pointing to a glass enclosure the size of a passenger van located next to the sealed room. "The shrinking process is very quick, taking less than a minute…"

"Will it hurt?" Scarlett asked, locking her arm around Champe's as if seeking protection.

"Some individuals experience slight nausea, maybe a tinge of dizziness," Eric explained.

"Just close your eyes during the process," Burke suggested.

"Good idea," Eric reiterated. "Most people that experience discomfort, that complain about the procedure, say the experience is similar to motion sickness. This is probably from the rapid change in your visual surroundings."

"Again, close your eyes," Burke said. "I do."

Scarlett smiled then looked to Champe for reassurance. He smiled in return and the two redirected their attention back to Eric.

"Once you reach optimal size," Eric continued, "Burke will lead you to the tram…"

"Tram? Like at the airport?" Champe asked, staring at the chamber.

"Just like at the airport except ours is far smaller," Eric said, laughing. "It will take you through two airlocks then to the door into the hunting area."

"The door opens roughly forty yards from camp," Burke explained. "The cook and your videographer are already there and waiting for us."

"Once you're in the field, as they say," Eric smiled, "the table will lift the hunt area upward and toward the skylight. The environment is climate controlled…"

"About 83 degrees," Burke offered.

"The special glass of the skylight ensures you get a natural sky, sunlight, etc. without dramatic changes in temperature," Eric continued. "The only thing you won't get is rain."

"How big's the enclosure?" Champe asked. "I mean, how big will it seem to us?"

"About 350 acres," Burke replied. "Most of it tall grass. A few native plants. It'll appear to be a jungle though. Grasses will tower over a 100 feet."

Champe beamed in excitement. Scarlett clung tighter to his arm, her face showing the same enthusiasm.

"So when do we go?" Champe almost stuttered, unable to keep his excitement at bay.

"No time like the present," Burke offered. "If you're ready that is."

"Hell yeah!" Champe almost exploded. "Hell yeah."

10.

Scarlett held tight around Champe's waist and chest. Despite the clear glass wall and door before her, Scarlett found the chamber she was sealed in to be claustrophobic. Sterile and intimidating. The walls were bright white plastic and the array of lenses and lights above her frightening.

"I don't know if I can do this," Scarlett mumbled.

"It'll be fine," Champe assured her before turning to Burke. "How many times have you done this?"

"Too many," Burke offered. He noticed Scarlett needed more and said, "It'll be fine. You won't feel a thing. Just close your eyes. When I tell you to open them, we'll head to that door and into the tram."

"That? Where?" Scarlett said, waving her hands in the direction that Burke had pointed. "I don't see anything. Let alone a door…"

"You'll see it up close and personal in about 20 seconds," Burke said gruffly. "Close your eyes…now."

"Now?!" Scarlett panicked. She vised her eyes tight and gripped into Champe with a force he'd never felt from her before. She saw a flash of blue from behind the darkness of her eyelids and felt Champe's hand cinch her waist. She had the feeling of falling and her stomach dropped as if she was riding a roller coaster.

"We're good," Burke offered from the darkness. "Let's pack it up."

"Open your eyes, babe," Champe whispered softly. "It's over."

Scarlett slowly opened her eyes then gazed in disbelief at her new surroundings. The walls of the sealed chamber appeared hundreds of stories tall. The floor seemed to go on forever and the lights and lenses she'd thought were so imposing just moments earlier were now a sky away.

"Pretty unreal, huh?" Burke smirked. "Let's get y'all's stuff loaded and I'll show you something that will really blow your mind."

"You OK?" Burke asked Scarlett.

Scarlett took a second to collect herself then offered, "Yeah. I just feel like I got off a ride at an amusement park is all."

"That'll pass," Burke promised.

Burke led them across the floor to the first airlock. He opened it with a control on his iPad and they entered a small tunnel that looked the same as the chamber minus the glass wall and strange lights. The lock behind them shut and the one before them opened. Burke led them through and onto the tram. They placed their luggage on the floor at the rear of the tram then sat. Burke pressed a button on his tablet and the doors shut and the tram took off.

"Bert," Burke said into his radio. "We'll be at the gate in 10. And bring the cart. We've got a lot of luggage. A lot."

Scarlett smiled for the first time since the procedure and said, "It's not that much luggage."

11.

Burke led Champe and Scarlett out of the tram and onto a small platform. They approached another airlock and made their way inside. The lock behind them closed and the door before them opened into a small landing. Burke led them across this and to a large steel door.

"You ready?" Burke smirked.

"Been waiting for it," Champe assured him.

Scarlett nodded and smiled from ear to ear.

The door parted and the three were immediately overcome with natural sunlight and the smell of fresh air. Their eyes adjusted to the brightness and they walked into the hunt area. The door behind them sealed and Bert and Andrew stepped forward to meet them. Burke made introductions and Bert smiled at Champe's and Scarlett's state of joyous bliss.

"Something, isn't it?" Bert offered, waving his hands to the jungle behind him.

"It's amazing," Scarlett almost cooed. "Utterly amazing."

"Let's get you to camp," Burke instructed. "Bert. Andrew. Get the luggage, will ya? There's a lot of it."

Champe laughed and led Scarlett after Burke and down the dirt path and through the thorn-covered trees that seemed to grow upwards of 100 feet. Scarlett registered the heat and rolled the sleeves of her shirt upward and unbuttoned yet another button at the front of her shirt that exposed even more of her surgically enhanced cleavage. Champe smiled in her direction and winked and continued leading her behind Burke.

They entered a clearing that held what Scarlett thought looked like the set from some old safari movie. There were five huge canvas tents each with a wood slat front porch. The camp also held a fire pit, outdoor kitchen, and a complete dining room set up under a 10-foot by 20-foot fly. There were canvas chairs situated around the fly and unlit gas lanterns on poles marking the path to each tent.

"This first tent serves as an office, storage, pantry, and communications center," Burke offered as they passed the first structure. "The next three are where Bert, Andrew, and I'll be staying… And this one over here will be yours."

Burke led them down the path to the most isolated tent and the only one to be elevated. They climbed the two-story stairs of the stilt frame and Burke gestured for Champe and Scarlett to enter first. They did and Scarlett was immediately overcome by its appointments. There was a king-sized bed, armoire, small sitting area, and a full-size bathroom with a claw foot tub and full shower. The tent was outfitted with screened windows, a ceiling fan, and air conditioning, all surrounded by a wraparound porch.

"I'll let you two get situated," Burke said, motioning for Bert and Andrew to drop the luggage at the foot of the bed. "What you do after that is up to you. Bert can whip up a late lunch, some cocktails, we can start hunting…"

"We'll be hunting," Champe exclaimed. "I'm ready now."

"It's your call," Burke reiterated. "We'll be around the office tent I showed you. Come on down when you're ready."

Burke led Bert and Andrew out of the tent and down the stairs. Scarlett pulled the sash that held the front flap open and the flaps closed. She leaned in and kissed Champe deeply and ran her hands over his chest and to his top shirt button. She undid the button and dropped her hands to the one below it.

"What are you doing?" Champe asked, thinking about the hunt at hand instead of the actions she was performing.

"The man said to get situated," Scarlett cooed on the tail end of a kiss. "I'm getting ready to situate you right where I want you."

12.

Champe and Scarlett made their way to the office tent to meet Burke. Scarlett had changed into a different, albeit similar, outfit than the one she wore upon arriving in the hunt area and Champe was fully dressed for the hunt. He wore gaiters over his boots, an ammo belt and sheath knife around his waist, and carried his double rifle over his shoulder. Bert approached them first with the offer of a cold drink or cocktail. Scarlett replied that she'd have an ice water with lime. Champe said that he'd wait until after the hunt to drink.

"I've got a cooler full of beer in the truck for when that time comes," Burke offered, exiting the office tent. "I was just talking to Eric. We are now under the skylight and ready for a full weekend of uninterrupted fun."

Champe and Scarlett both looked upward then to each other.

"I can't tell there's glass above us," Champe offered. "Unbelievable."

Burke looked to Scarlett and asked if she wanted anything added to the cooler. She requested water, said that she looked forward to a cold beer as well then took the glass of ice water with lime from Bert when he returned. She offered thanks, drank from the glass then turned back to Burke.

"We'll load up and make our way to the hunting area," Burke explained. "We'll look for tracks, sign, spoor. Proceed on foot if we see anything worth checking out."

"Sounds good!" Champe said.

Andrew drove a converted Toyota Tacoma 4 x 4 truck around and to just in front of the office tent. The four-door truck had a raised bench seat in the bed, industrial front and rear bumpers, a winch, LED lights directed front and back, a spotlight, gun racks, and action cameras mounted throughout. Andrew exited the truck and said to Burke, "She's all yours."

"Champe, I'll ask that you and Scarlett ride in the raised seat. View's better up there. Put your rifle in the rack mounted before it. Next to mine," Burke instructed. "Andrew usually stands behind where y'all will be."

Andrew nodded then held out two nylon-webbed chest harnesses. "Can I ask y'all to wear these GoPros? I'll download the footage at the end of each day."

Champe nodded and put the harness on so the camera was situated pointing outward from his sternum. Scarlett struggled with hers then looked to Andrew for assistance. Andrew noted the camera sitting atop her cleavage, smiled, then looked to Champe who laughed and said, "I got ya, babe." He tightened the straps and sat the camera so it faced forward.

"Does it ruin my look?" Scarlett asked.

"There's still plenty to look at," Champe assured her.

Andrew climbed into the truck bed and clicked into a belted harness that allowed him to ride hands free while holding a camera over his shoulder standing in the back of a moving truck.

"I'll film from back here," Andrew explained. "And follow you when you're on foot. The action cameras we're all wearing plus the ones on the truck will allow me to put together a fantastic keepsake for you."

"How will I know if I can shoot or not?" Champe asked, climbing into the truck bed.

"I'll tell you when..." Burke started.

"No. No. No," Champe corrected. "I mean in regards to whether Andrew will get my shot on film. I don't want him to miss my money shot."

Scarlett raised one eyebrow in Champe's direction at his saying "money shot" and took his hand and climbed into the truck bed.

"Burke and I have worked together. A lot." Andrew chuckled. "We can almost read each other's thoughts…"

"And dammit if Andrew's ain't dirty," Burke chuckled.

Andrew laughed and said, "I always let Burke know if I need a better line of sight. I've never missed a money shot. I won't with you either. Promise."

"Enough talks about money shots and camera angles," Burke barked from the cab. "Let's go kill some bugs!"

13.

Burke started the truck and the engine roared to life. He put the vehicle in gear and headed down the dirt road that led out of camp. He stopped the vehicle 15 yards from an electrified gate that stood twenty feet tall. He pressed a command on his iPad and the gate opened inward. He drove through and waited for the gate to shut then continued onward.

"One more to go," Andrew said.

Champe turned around and asked, "What?"

"We've got two electric fences surrounding the camp," Andrew explained. "Well, half the camp actually. The wall of the enclosure serves as the barrier behind camp."

Burke reached the second gate, opened it, and drove through. He waited for it to close then drove forward.

"Why is there a fence at all?" Scarlett asked Andrew. "I mean, don't you only put in the bugs that you're gonna shoot? There aren't extra out here? Are there?"

"No," Andrew assured her. "We only place the number and species the hunter plans to take. In Champe's case, that's…"

"Seven total," Champe exclaimed.

"Okay. Seven," Andrew parroted. "But that's seven insects in the reserve. We only hunt one at a time. That means the rest are out here wandering who knows where. The last thing we want is for a hungry ant to wander into camp while we're sleeping."

Scarlett nodded and fought her wind-blown hair into a tight ponytail. "Has that ever happened? One come into camp?"

"Only once that I know of," Andrew admitted. "A tarantula hawk…"

"Holy shit!" Champe barked in disbelief. "A tarantula hawk? Really?"

"Yes, sir, a tarantula hawk. Or spider wasp. Whatever you want to call it. He was de-winged," Andrew explained before bursting into laughter. "He hit the fence around two in the morning and oh my God did he stink! Several thousand pounds of electric-fried bug. Just nasty. Absolutely horrid."

Champe and Scarlett laughed at Andrew's visuals and Burke reacted to the joyfulness coming from the truck bed. "What the hell's so funny?" he barked. "You're supposed to be looking for signs!"

"Will do, good sir," Andrew cried over the wind. He turned his head to the ground passing by and said to Scarlett, "You've never seen sand like that before. Very, very few have."

Scarlett looked down to witness a sea of white rocks and boulders. Among this flood of white were stones of rose and pink, topaz and violet. The ground sparkled and reflected the light in ways she'd never seen before.

"What is all that?" she exclaimed. "Diamonds and jewels?"

"That's just what sand looks like when you're knee-high to an ant." Andrew laughed, making sure to get Scarlett's reaction on video.

They drove onward and into an area where the grass grew high above the road and bathed all that was below it in a permanent dusk. The grass was of the same variety Champe has seen during his cinema hunt but far larger and more grandiose. The trunks were half the size of sequoias, covered in vivid diamond-shaped scales, and thorns that jutted outward and upward like inverted scimitars. Champe and Scarlett were totally enthralled by their surroundings. They couldn't believe what they were seeing and they loved it.

A sudden explosion rocked the vehicle sideways and to the right of the road. Champe and Scarlett were thrown against the side railing of the raised seat and Andrew jerked hard, his safety strap cutting into him. The engine whined to a halt. Burke barked obscenities. The truck rocked again and slammed into a massive blade of grass, one of its monster-sized thorns coming centimeters from piercing Scarlett's head. The vehicle shook and Andrew fought to stand. He made it to his feet, pointed his camera at the front passenger door, and muttered in disbelief.

"Oh. My. God."

Burke fought to start the truck. The engine ground and sputtered. Champe pulled himself off Scarlett and stood. He shot his hand out to help Scarlett stand then turned toward the front cab.

"Holy shit!"

Scarlett saw the dread in Champe's eyes.

Her hand fell as his grip ceased.

Champe fought to keep his footing atop the violently shaking truck. He reached for his rifle in the rack but each sudden jar from the vehicle's rapid lurch jostled the gun and his hand in opposite directions. The truck cranked and the engine roared to life. Burke screamed, "Hold on!" and ground the gear into place. The truck jumped backward then was pulled forward. It sped backward once more then was pulled forward. Burke barked, "Come on, Goddammit!" and gunned the engine. The truck exploded backward. Tires spun. Stones and rocks of every color spit upward. The tires caught and the truck jumped backward with rocket thrust.

Scarlett clawed to her feet and clung to the rifle rack before the seat in order to stand. Champe was still fighting to retrieve his rifle. Scarlett looked forward to see a massive beast, twice the size of an elephant, thrashing its head violently from side to side in apparent effort to remove the truck door that sat lodged on its horn. It was a blur of violence painted in soft hues of aquamarine and the darkest of black. Beautiful savagery in motion.

"What the…?" Scarlett muttered in disbelief.

"I think it's my Western Hercules Beetle," Champe shot back.

The truck's tail-end fishtailed then slammed into a blade of grass. Champe, Scarlett, and Andrew were thrown forward and against the rifle rack. A tire-sized thorn fell from the vegetation, barely missing Andrew and denting the truck bed with the force of a thunderclap. Burke blew out of the front cab and climbed halfway into the bed to retrieve his rifle.

"Let's go!" Burke commanded in Champe's direction. "Now!"

Champe looked ahead to see the gigantic beetle repeatedly slamming the car door still lodged on its head horn into blades of grass in an effort to dislodge it.

"Today, Champe!" Burke howled.

Champe grabbed his rifle and jumped from the truck bed to the ground below. Andrew unsnapped his harness, ensured his camera was still intact, and followed.

"What about …?" Scarlett cried out.

"Stay in the truck!" Burke shot back. "Better view of the show."

Scarlett feigned pouting then stood atop the raised seat and stared at the winding road before.

"How far—?" Champe started to ask.

"Maybe eighty yards," Burke muttered. He ran his hands over his salt and pepper facial stubble in thought. He'd never approached more than 25,000 pounds of pissed-off beetle fighting a passenger-side door attached to its face before and wasn't exactly sure of the best approach. Normally, he'd go for the brain shot, but there was a car door acting as a shield in front of it. The beetle's heart ran the length of its body and just below the elytron but given the thrashing about this thing was doing, getting a clean shot might be next to impossible. Not to mention the adrenaline that must be coursing through that beast. So much that piercing its brain or snapping its elongated heart in half would only piss it off.

The beast swung the truck door into a towering blade of grass once more. The force of repeated contact finally gave way and the animal's bottom horn snapped off with a deafening crack that echoed down the road and over Burke, Champe, and Andrew. The enraged monstrosity let loose a high-pitched shrill of pain and clawed at the dirt in anger. Burke took four bullets from his ammo belt. He placed two in the palm and two in the fingers of his left hand. Champe saw this and did the same with ammo from his own belt. The herculean-sized beetle raised its head and swept its antennae back and forth in pure rage. It clawed the dirt before it found purchase and lunged forward at breakneck speed.

"Shit," Burke moaned. "Hit 'em in the head with everything ya got!"

Burke fired his .600 N.E. A yellowish-orange flame shot outward and the sound of thunder clapped. The bullet struck the beast just under the pronotal horn that jutted from the top of its pronotum, or head. The beast wobbled slightly but seemed seemingly unfazed. Champe fired next, hitting the beast in the actual pronotal horn. Burke fired once more. Then Champe. Both men reloaded with breakneck speed and fired twice more. Each then reloaded again.

The beetle closed the distance to twenty yards. Burke fired for the fifth then sixth time, each bullet slamming into the creature's head. Champe continued the barrage, his fifth bullet hitting and breaking off the monster's pronotal horn. The beast fell forward, its momentum plowing it through the earth and toward the three adventurers. Burke grabbed Champe by the arm and pulled him to their right. Andrew followed in haste. The monstrous insect slid to a stop and Burke pointed to a point on the elytron.

"Hit 'em in the heart," Burke ordered.

Champe obeyed and the creature bucked in an involuntary reaction to the impact.

"Hit 'em again!" Burke barked. "Then reload."

Champe did as ordered and fired a total of three more times into the beast's heart. He began to reload his massive rifle once more then ceased to take Burke's outstretched hand.

"Good job," Burke congratulated. "Damn nice."

14.

Scarlett ran over and vaulted herself into Champe's arms. He held her tight and spun her around as he kissed her. He dropped her to her feet and stared at the pure excitement in her eyes.

"That was incredible," Scarlett assured him in a shaky voice. "But I thought y'all were dead! Gonna be dead! Oh my God, I couldn't believe it!"

"I… I can't describe it," Champe stuttered on heavy adrenaline. "It was…like time just slowed…"

"Ya did good," Burke reiterated. "Damn good."

Andrew held his camera aloft and boasted, "And I got it all on video! All of it! Damn. The end result is gonna be fantastic!"

Burke slapped Andrew on the back in praise. "Good job, sir."

"How's your arm?" Scarlett cooed as she ran her fingers over his bicep and up his shoulder.

"I'll be feeling it tomorrow, for sure," Andrew admitted.

"Probably not 'til the safari's over," Burke offered. "Then it'll feel like a mule kicked you in your sleep."

"Let's get some trophy pics," Andrew instructed. "Then I'll grab y'all some beers… Shit! Is the truck alright?"

All turned to look at the truck still wedged against the enormous blade of grass. The tailgate of the Toyota was partially smashed in. There was a dent from where a huge grass thorn had crashed into the bed, and the passenger door had been ripped from the vehicle, leaving only a twisted frame and sheared-off hinges.

"She ain't pretty. That's for sure," Burke admitted. "Motor died when we slammed into the tree. I'm sure it'll crank over again though. We'll get the pictures first then I'll check her out while we have some cold ones."

Andrew staged a number of trophy pictures. He took some of just Champe and the beetle, some with Champe and Scarlett in front of the beetle, and some with just Champe and Burke in front of the beetle. Normally, when there was a couple on a safari, Andrew would get a picture of the two with the Professional Hunter in front of the kill. But Andrew decided not to stage such a picture on this trip. The last thing he wanted to do was to put his friend Burke in a picture with their boss's wife and her boy toy.

There'd be no way to explain that one.

He decided playing dumb as to who the woman was would be his best course of action.

At least until after the safari.

After the pictures were completed, Burke, Champe, Scarlett, and Andrew returned to the truck. The three men stowed their rifles and camera while Scarlett took it upon herself to dig some cold beers out of the cooler. Luckily, none of the glass bottles had been damaged during the multiple vehicle wrecks. Each person took a bottle of Sol then clinked the bottles and raised them in toast.

"To a great first kill," Burke toasted. "Congrats!"

They all toasted and drank and leaned against the truck in an attempt to allow the adrenaline they'd all accumulated ease out of their systems.

"So, tell me," Champe began. "And be honest. Did you know that'd be the first bug we'd encounter?"

"Absolutely not," Burke assured Champe, slightly annoyed at the question. "The bugs were put in the day you told me what you wanted to hunt. I have no idea where they go after the tech boys drop them in. My job's to find them. It just so happened that this one found us first."

"Why'd you think he charged us?" Scarlett asked.

"Probably thought we were another beetle," Burke theorized. "Maybe he smelled us."

"Speaking of smelling us," Andrew began. "This boy's getting pretty ripe. Whatcha say we move on down the road?"

"Yeah, he stinks!" Scarlett agreed, holding her nose as if she couldn't take the smell.

"That's what happens when you put their insides on their outsides," Champe said, laughing.

Scarlett feigned shock and swatted Champe's chest.

"Only problem is that he's in the road," Burke stated. "The road splits up beyond his body but the road behind us leads straight back to camp. We'll have to winch him outta the road so we can get by."

"I'll let y'all handle that," Scarlett assured them.

15.

The truck started on the second attempt.

Burke put the truck in gear and drove toward the fallen beetle. He stopped 15 feet from the carcass, put the truck in park, disengaged the winch, and walked to the front of the vehicle where Andrew stood.

"Whatcha think?" Andrew asked, pulling the hook and cable from the winch.

Burke studied the monstrosity before him. It was huge. At more than 25,000 pounds in weight, there was no way to actually drag the thing out of the road. He'd burn the truck's transmission up trying to do so. He just needed to drag it far enough to one side of the road or the other in order to be able to drive the truck around it.

"We could cable around his bottom horn," Champe interrupted Burke's train of thought.

"I don't think there's enough horn left," Andrew offered. "He ripped most of it off when he slammed the car door off of it."

Burke walked to the right of the beast, then to the left.

"Let's hook on his front leg here," Burke instructed. He then pointed to an area behind the vehicle. "I'll drag him to the side by backing in between those two blades of grass. That should give us enough room to drive around him on the left."

Champe walked to the left side of the beetle to have a look. "That should work," he offered.

Andrew wrapped the hook around the beetle's front leg and cinched the cable tight. Burke got into the truck and pulled in the winch until the cable went taut with tension. He put the truck in reverse and eased on the gas. The truck lurched backward then jerked to a halt. Burke pressed harder on the gas and the tires dug deeper then found purchase. The Toyota strained but pulled the goliath back and to the side of the road. Burke released the winch and walked to the front of the vehicle. Andrew and Champe released the hook from the beetle's leg and dropped the cable to the ground so Burke could winch it in.

"What now?" Scarlett asked, taking Champe's hand into hers.

"Be quiet!" Burke suddenly barked.

Scarlett's face scrunched in disbelief. She jerked a look toward Champe then said, "Are you gonna—?"

"Hush! Now!" Burke insisted. He walked back to the truck and grabbed his rifle. He turned back toward the hunting party that stood before the fallen elephantine beetle. Champe and Scarlett stared at Burke in disbelief. Andrew looked at Burke for some sign or instruction. The air was suddenly pierced by a deafening stridulating chirp. Scarlett cringed and put her hands to her ears. Andrew ran to get his camera from the truck bed.

The bullet ant came to rest on top of the beetle, landing with such force that hemolymph exploded from every bullet hole and the ground shook. Champe jerked his head around and upward to see the ant's head only 10 feet above him. Scarlett screamed in sheer panic. Champe grabbed Scarlett's hand and began pulling her toward the truck. The ant opened its mandibles with a shrieking hiss and lunged forward. It landed on the ground just behind Scarlett. The force of the ant's impact just behind her knocked Scarlett off her feet and she stumbled and fell. Champe fought to pull her to her feet but Burke pushed him over and out of his way with a heavy swipe of his double rifle.

Burke fired almost point blank into the ant's head.

Then fired again.

Hemolymph and other intestinal fluids bespattered everywhere. Champe fought his way to his feet then pulled the hysterically screaming Scarlett upward. Burke fired twice more and the ant collapsed at his feet with a deafening thud that kicked up rocks and dirt.

16.

Scarlett took the beer that Champe handed her from the cooler. It was ice cold and went down easily. A little too easily but then Scarlett was really hoping it'd kill her adrenaline rush.

She needed to calm down.

She needed to calm down and talk herself out of being the scared frail woman she'd just turned into.

But how could she have not turned into such? After all, an ant half the size of an elephant had almost jumped on top of her. It had almost grabbed her in its jaws.

Or whatever those jaw things were.

Yes, she had screamed.

She'd screamed in panic then collapsed into metaphorical jelly. Now the three men around her were looking at her to see if she was going to ruin their fun. If she was going to burst into tears and whine and tell Champe to get her back to normal size and back into the normal world.

She downed a third of her beer in one gulp and came back up with a slight belch. She wiped her mouth with the back of her hand and pulled what little strength she had from deep inside her.

"Thanks for the fast thinking, Burke," Scarlett said, her voice still shaky. "I thought I was a goner."

"You okay, babe?" Champe asked.

"Yep," Scarlett quipped. "Just need to come down some."

Burke looked annoyed. He wasn't buying her act for a second. She was scared to death. But, she had managed to pull it together pretty quick. Burke wiped the sweat from his brow and said to Champe, "It's your safari. Your call. If she's rattled and wants to leave, I can put the call in right now and we'd be outta here within the hour."

"I'm fine," Scarlett insisted. "I assure you of that. I'm no more rattled than anyone else that just had an ant try to kill her would be."

Champe and Andrew smiled at Scarlett's boldness.

"It's up to you," Burke reiterated. "Y'all's call."

Champe looked in Scarlett's eyes. She nodded that she was fine and Champe turned back to Burke.

"We're good," Champe assured Burke. "But why don't we call it a day? Head back to camp."

"We can do that," Burke said.

"We don't have to," Scarlett insisted. "Really, I'm good."

"I know," Champe exclaimed. "But we had allotted two animals…er, bugs for today and we got two. Day's over."

"You got one," Burke corrected. "I saved you from this one."

"You sure did that." Champe smirked. "Thanks."

"Yes, thank you, Burke," Scarlett offered.

"I got the whole thing on camera," Andrew excitedly promised. "Everything from when the ant appeared up until when Burke dropped him. Gonna make a spectacular video. Especially once I intercut it with the footage from all of your action cameras."

"I know what else this ant will make," Burke insisted. He placed his rifle in the rear gun rack and pulled an axe from the truck's toolbox. He carried the axe over to the ant and stared down at its front leg.

17.

"I can't believe how freakin' awesome this is!" Scarlett said, taking another huge bite of ant meat. "Congratulations, Bert. You really know how to cook!" Bert smiled and raised his wine glass. Burke, Champe, Scarlett, and Andrew held their drinks aloft. "To family and friends and the adventure at hand," Bert toasted.

Glasses clinked, people agreed, then returned to the food and conversation.

"It really tastes like king crab. I just can't believe it," Champe declared. He cracked another ant leg, removed the meat with a seafood fork, and plunged it into the bowl of lemon butter before him. He devoured the butter-soaked chunk in one bite and said again, "King crab. Tastes exactly like king crab."

"I think it's more like lobster," Scarlett exclaimed, motioning for Champe to pass her more lemon slices.

"I agree with you." Burke nodded in Scarlett's direction. "It's more like lobster."

"I think it tastes like a mixture of both meats," Andrew exclaimed.

Scarlett laughed and joked, "What are you a politician? Give us a real answer."

"No. I do. I think it tastes like a mixture of both," Andrew insisted. "A politician. Ha! That'll be the day."

"Have y'all eaten anything else?" Champe asked of Burke. "Like that beetle we got. What do they taste like?"

Burke killed his wine then motioned for Bert to grab him a tequila. Bert nodded and stood from the table.

"Anyone else?" Bert asked. "More wine? Beer? Liquor?"

The group gave their orders and Bert headed back toward the bar in the dining tent to retrieve the drinks. The group was eating outside, enjoying the stars above and climate-controlled air. It was 78 degrees and perfectly comfortable for outdoor dining.

"What does beetle taste like?" Burke stated the question once more. "I'd have to say…shit. That sound about right, Andrew?"

Andrew laughed and agreed. "That's about as good a description as I could come up with. It tastes like complete and total shit."

The table burst into laughter and everyone finished their drinks. Bert returned with a tray full of requested drinks and handed them out individually.

"Bert," Scarlett began. "Burke and Andrew swear that beetle tastes like shit. Is this true?"

Bert burst into laughter and said, "Yes. Beetle tastes like shit. And believe me, I tried every cooking trick of the trade I could think of to no avail. The meat is just terrible no matter what you do to it."

"Of course, we were eating dung beetle," Burke said dryly. "I mean, it eats shit. Not sure why we were surprised to find that it tastes like what it'd been eating."

Champe and Scarlett looked to each other then burst into heavy laughter. Andrew and Bert followed and soon all at the table were doubled over at Burke's realization.

"Is that true?" Scarlett asked through fits of laughter. "Was the one you tried a dung beetle? Really?"

"Oh yeah," Burke joked. "Pulled him straight off a cow patty, tossed him into the reserve here, killed him, n' let Bert there throw him in the oven."

"I don't believe you." Scarlett giggled. "Not one bit."

"Good," Bert exclaimed. "Cuz Burke is the one's that full of shit…"

"Yeah, but would I taste like that if you cooked me?" Burke smiled.

"Probably!" Bert assured him. "Probably!"

18.

Maria adjusted her blonde wig in the mirror.

She was dressed in a purposely ill-fitting pantsuit that allowed her to carry a pistol, ammo, and compact retractable baton. She wore glasses and heavy makeup to complete her disguise. This display was perhaps a slight bit of overkill but she couldn't take a chance. It was better to let Eric see what she wanted to project than for him to see her in her regular state.

Maria clipped the I.D. tag that displayed her picture in the wig, glasses, and heavy makeup and the name of "Elizabeth Allen" to her jacket. She took one last look in the mirror, nodded, then exited the bathroom.

Her drive to the tech campus was a short one even with the Friday night traffic. She used her self-issued fake I.D. badge to enter the front gate, parked in the lot closest to the main building then made her way to the lab. Eric was sitting at a computer terminal playing an online game when she entered.

"Hello," Maria announced.

Eric jumped in his seat. His chair rolled back and away from the terminal and he thought about standing up but thought the better of it. He put his hand to his chest as if trying to keep his rapidly beating heart from exploding through it.

"Jeeze!" Eric chuckled. "You scared the crap outta me."

"I'm sorry. I certainly didn't mean to." Maria smiled. She walked toward Eric and held out her hand. "I'm Elizabeth Allen. I'm your replacement for the weekend."

"Replacement?" Eric asked. He was drawing a blank. What was she talking about?

"Yes. Did Human Resources not contact you?"

Eric looked around the room as if the contact the attractive woman before him was speaking about might be floating in the air somewhere.

"I guess not," Eric stuttered through nervous laughter. "Cuz... I don't know what you're talking about."

"It's just you tonight, correct?"

"Yeah..."

"Because Alex was told by H.R. that he had accrued too many weekends?"

"Yeah..."

"Apparently, you have as well," Maria explained. "H.R. was supposed to let you know."

Eric scratched his head in thought and disbelief. He thought back to how many weekends he'd worked in the past six months. Quite a few. Burke had taken a lot of clients on safari in the past half year. Not that Eric minded working on weekends. He didn't really care. The only difference between working a weekend and staying at home for the weekend was the computer he played online games on.

"They didn't tell me. I mean, nobody told me," Eric explained. "But I really don't mind. I mean, I've already got my regular couch down the hall already made up and everything."

"I'm just doing what I was told," Maria countered. "I was assigned to monitor Mr. Tyler and his clients' safari and to call Alex if an emergency should arise."

"Yeah, Alex did tell me he'd be around if I needed to call," Eric said.

"See." Maria smiled. "There you have it. Alex told you he was on call. He just didn't tell you I'd be the one calling him if need be."

Eric stood in thought.

Maria continued.

"I'm familiar with the communication system. I actually helped Alex monitor a hunt once while you were out ill...was it last February?"

Eric thought for a moment. "Oh yeah. I was out with a stomach bug. Real nasty."

"I'm sure." Maria smiled.

Eric gave into the idea that Maria was his replacement and that Alex and Human Resources had somehow failed to inform him of such. He told Maria he'd collect his things then be on his way. He smiled and went down the hall to the office where his favorite couch was, stripped it of its linens, and made his way to the parking lot.

19.

After Maria watched Eric exit the building on the security camera, she entered the control sequence that would lower the hunt area back to table level. She exited the office and walked to the insectary.

The room smelled stale and slightly of disinfectant, and its shelves were lined with container after container of insects. Some were held in terrariums, others in plastic containers, and some even in paper envelopes. Maria scanned the shelves then collected several small containers and returned to the lab. The hunt area, although not fully lowered, was now easily accessible. Maria carried the six small containers to the far side of the table and emptied the insects from each into the area that was opposite from the safari camp. She set the controls to raise the hunt area back to the skylight and turned to see Eric standing in the doorway.

"I forgot my keys," Eric mumbled.

Maria walked from behind the clear plastic sheeting that separated the lab from the hunt area. Eric saw the area behind her slowly rising and the plastic containers in her hands.

"What are you... What did you do?" he stammered in disbelief. "Are those insect containers? Did you...?"

Eric walked toward the hunt area in confusion and disbelief.

"Does Burke know what you...that you...?" Eric dropped his train of thought and changed course and headed instead to the bank or radios situated next to the computer he'd played a game on only a few minutes earlier. "I better call..."

Maria crossed the room in breakneck speed. She dropped the plastic containers and pulled the compacted baton from her belt.

She flung it open and brought it down on Eric's arm as he reached for a radio. His arm snapped and he recoiled it pain and utter confusion, shock, and disbelief. Tears welled in his eyes and all he could think to say was, "Why?"

Maria grabbed the hair on the back of Eric's head and drove him forward and toward the glass doors that held the shrink technology. Eric tried to fight her control but the pain of his arm was too much and he felt lightheaded and his feet stumbled to keep up with her. Maria slammed Eric's face into the glass door with such force that it smashed his nose and split his lip. Blood flowered across the glass door then painted a streak downward as Eric fell to his knees. Maria opened the doors then took Eric by the hair once more and pulled him from his knees. She threw him into the chamber then sealed the doors.

Eric fell against the far wall of the chamber then collapsed onto the floor. His face was a painting of tears, snot, and blood and he spit to clear his mouth. He took in a deep breath and cringed at the pain his arm was causing him. He looked toward the ceiling just as the room was bathed in a sharp blue light.

20.

Maria walked from the shrink controls to the radio bank. She unplugged their chargers and took the battery from each individual radio and placed them in her pocket. From there, she moved onto the Internet connection. She pulled the ether cables and unplugged the power sources. She walked to the breaker that controlled the power to the hunt area and inner lab and closed the circuit. She deleted the security footage from that day and left.

21.

Eric opened his eyes to a white expanse. The floor of the shrink chamber went to the horizon, the walls seemed days away, and it would take a helicopter to reach the ceiling. He looked out the glass doors to see the lab shrouded in darkness. There were no overhead lights on, no desk lamps, and no computer displays.

He struggled through the pain to assess his situation.

What had just happened?

And why?

A woman had come in telling him to leave, giving him reasons that in hindsight seemed rather vague.

But before that...

Before that, Alex was told not to come in for the weekend.

Then he was told to leave and that this woman, Elizabeth, would handle things. He had left as instructed but forgot his keys. He did that all the time. Especially when frazzled or rushed. He returned to get his keys only to see Elizabeth in the hunt room. The table was going up, which means that she had lowered it for some reason. She exited the room with insect cages.

Had she put more insects in the hunt area?

Did Burke instruct her to do so?

No.

Probably not.

Regardless, why did she attack him and leave him a shrunken mess?

Eric knew there was no way to exit the shrinking chamber other than have someone return him to normal size—which wasn't going to happen—or to take the tram to the hunt area.

He decided that was his best chance.

He'd take the tram to the hunt area. They had a first-aid kit there and Burke knew enough emergency care to help him with his arm. Also, Burke might know what was going on.

And he had communications to call the outside world.

Eric rose to his feet and made his way to the tram door. Realizing he didn't have an iPad, he worked the manual controls to open the airlock. He passed through both locks then boarded the tram. The tram lurched forward and Eric held his arm in pain. He was hit with another bolt of pain when the tram came to a stop. He grimaced and exited the tram and made his way to the final airlock. He passed through both locks and to the realization and remembrance that the hunt area was no longer there.

It had been raised.

The airlock now opened out to nothing but a small landing.

The hunt area was thousands of feet above him, the ground hundreds of feet below.

Eric turned to open the airlock then remembered there were no controls on his side that would allow him back in. The ability to open the lock could only be controlled from the door on the other side of the hunt area or via an iPad he didn't have. He looked out at the lab once more and wept. The pain was too much. The realization that he was basically stuck on a cliff with no way off was too much.

He gave up.

He collapsed with his back against the airlock door and sobbed.

22.

"It's ready," Scarlett called to Champe.

Champe walked from the bed to the bathroom of the tent to find Scarlett sitting in an overflowing bubble bath. The bathroom was lit by several candles and smelled of the lavender bubble bath she had apparently used to create such a cloud of bubbles. She handed him an open beer and he eased into the water behind her.

"Damn, that's hot," he complained.

"It'll cool off," she countered.

Champe took a long pull off his beer and placed it on the table next to the bath. He looked out the screened wall to the forest below and beyond. The camp was illuminated by a path of gas lanterns and the sky above the tall grasses lit by a million stars. It was beautiful.

But also alien.

While he appreciated the beauty of the place, his subconscious struggled with the reality of it all. Was the forest before him really composed of grass that would normally fall short of his ankle? Was the rhino-sized beast that almost caught Scarlett in its pinchers really just an ant? Champe took another drink and tried to put all thoughts out of his head. He just wanted to relax and to enjoy what was coming his way.

Scarlett leaned forward then turned to face Champe. She took a drink of wine then asked Champe if his shoulder hurt. He said that it didn't then asked how she really felt about the ant attack.

"I'm fine," she said. "I mean, it scared the shit outta me. It still does when I think about it. But I'm trying to put it outta my mind.

There's no need to worry about things that have already happened. And speaking of worrying…"

Scarlett leaned in and kissed Champe then slinked back to her side of the tub, all the while making sure that the bubble hung on her in just the right way. She wanted to keep Champe interested.

"Did you notice that no one here knows who I am?" she boasted. "Just like I told ya."

Champe nodded and changed the subject. The last thing he wanted to talk about was her husband.

"Tomorrow's gonna be a long day," Champe informed her. "We're gonna hunt all day."

"I'm up for it," Scarlett exclaimed. "I'm ready for anything that comes our way!"

23.

Burke killed his tequila, threw his cigar butt in the remains of the campfire, and walked the lantern-lined path to his tent. He pulled back the flap, entered, and clicked the light switch.

Nothing.

He flicked it off then on again as if that was the problem.

Still nothing.

"Screw it," Burke mumbled.

He walked in the dark to his bed. He sat on the edge and removed his boots and placed them aside. He stripped down to his boxers, got under the sheets, and stared at the dark tent fabric above him.

Tomorrow was going to be a long day.

Very long.

They'd be in the field looking for and hopefully taking three insects. Hopefully, there'd be no more attacks on his clients. But that girl had rebounded pretty well. Far better than most gals he'd met during the course of his career. And Champe was actually a pretty good hunter and not near as much of a pain in his ass as he thought he'd be. He stayed calm in a crisis and seemed to know how to handle Scarlett.

Burke ended his nightly reflection by picturing himself on the shores of Lake Amistad. The sun was warm, the water a clear blue, and his drink cold. Maybe two more years of guiding and he'd be able to return and retire there.

To make the dream a reality.

But for now, it was a dream, literally and figuratively.

24.

Bert awoke to the call of nature.

At 46 years old, he found himself getting up two and three and sometimes even four times a night to urinate. Not one to face facts, especially when they were unflattering and directed towards him, Bert blamed this frequency of visits to the bathroom on his nightly alcohol consumption.

He climbed out of bed and made his way to the bathroom, pausing to look out the screened walls of what served as his "bedroom." The gas lanterns lining the trail painted the path in a soft amber glow, and the stars above bathed the forest beyond the electric fence in an almost romantic aurora. The camp was beautiful and he was fortunate to be a part of it.

He entered the door to the bathroom to the sound of heavy and repetitive clicking. He looked upward to identify the sound only to see the huge compound eyes of a praying mantis looking down at him. It was enormous, a literal nightmare incarnate.

And the last thing Bert would ever see.

The mantis pieced Bert's chest with its left leg spike and pinned him to the wooden floor. Bert screamed a guttural cry of terror that reverberated throughout the camp. Blood coughed up from his lungs and his brain fought not to give up what his body already knew.

He was dead.

25.

Burke shot out of bed like a man possessed.

He turned his ear toward the direction of the scream. He pulled his pants on, grabbed his rifle and his ammo belt, and ran to Bert's tent. He pulled back the canvas flap that served as the front door and entered with his rifle aimed before him. The sound of crushing bone and the heavy slurping of liquids echoed from the bathroom. Burke eased quietly through the tent and toward the bathroom door.

The mantis had crushed Bert's skull and was feasting on his brain. The beast saw Burke and pulled his leg spike from Bert's body and backed away. It tilted its head to get a better view of its challenger and crossed its front arms as if sharpening them against one another and lunged forward.

"You son of a bitch!"

Burke screamed and fired his rifle. The bullet slammed into the beast's chest and exploded outward from its back. Momentum of the attack fought against the impact of the bullet and the beast teetered to and fro in an effort to stand. Burke fired once more into the mantis' chest. The force of the bullet spun the apex predator around and it lunged forward in an effort to escape. Burke reloaded as the tent was pulled from its frame and carried away by the mantis. He fired once more but couldn't be sure if he hit the cloaked monster.

The mantis raged into a lantern on the trail and was rewarded with an explosion of fuel and flame. The canvas was engulfed in flames and the beast thrashed violently to escape the flames that were burning all around it. The tent flew off the mantis like a comet and landed at the edge of Andrew's tent. The fire jumped and the standing structure quickly became a frame of rapidly rising flames. Andrew dove from the fire into the sand and came to his feet coughing and struggling to see through his smoke-burnt eyes.

"Burke!" he screamed. "Burke!"

"Hang on!" Burke yelled over the melee of fire and a 17-foot tall mantis in the last throes of death. He aimed at the violently thrashing beast's center mass and fired. The mantis exploded backward and over, its impact with the ground sending upward dirt and stone, flame and viscera.

26.

"What the hell was that…?" Champe barked.

"Was that a scream?" Scarlett echoed.

Champe exploded from the bath and ran to the front of the tent. He pulled on a pair of pants sans boxers and ran to the front porch. Scarlett wrapped a towel around her and followed.

They looked down to see Burke run from his tent to Bert's.

"He's got his rifle," Scarlett stated. "Why does he have—?"

Scarlett's question was answered prematurely by the sudden boom of a .600 N.E. rifle shot. She screamed in shock and disbelief. Champe grabbed her around the shoulders just as a second gunshot echoed throughout the camp. Bert's tent exploded from its frame and floated outward and forward.

"What the hell?!" Champe asked of the chaos.

Burke appeared from the darkness and fired into the ever-moving wall of canvas. The tent was thrown backward and crashed into a lantern, igniting into a ball of flame that seemed to fight in every direction. The flaming mass split in two and only then did Champe and Scarlett see that it was a mantis flailing about in pain and partially on fire.

Andrew's tent suddenly burst into flames, and Scarlett screamed at the violent confusion unfolding below her.

"Get dressed!" Champe yelled as he bolted down the stairs and toward the sea of flames.

27.

"You okay?" Burke asked as he helped Andrew to his feet.

Andrew nodded and coughed, still struggling to breathe.

Burke left Andrew fighting for air and rushed to his tent to retrieve a fire extinguisher. He exited his tent and fought forward with the extinguisher in an effort to keep the flames from jumping to his. Andrew's tent collapsed in upon itself and the flames slowly died, giving way to smoldering coals of canvas and wood.

Champe ran to Andrew and asked his condition then turned to Burke as he approached with rifle in hand.

"Where's your—?" Burke started.

"Scarlett?" Champe finished. "Up in our tent."

"Go. Go now," Burke commanded. "Stay up there, rifle at the ready until I come up to get you. It's not safe down here."

"Why? What's going on?" Champe struggled to make sense of what was happening.

"I'm going to find out," Burke assured Champe. "Now, go. Go now!"

Champe ran toward his tent and Burke looked to Andrew.

"You need some oxygen?"

Andrew spit and said that he didn't then followed Burke to his tent. Burke flipped the light switch upon entering the cursed the darkness.

"Did you have any juice in your tent?"

"I dunno," Andrew answered with a small cough. "I didn't check before... Is Bert...?"

Burke nodded.

Andrew lowered his head and cursed.

Burke grabbed a flashlight from his side table and thrust it towards Andrew. Burke leaned over to a tactical case at the foot of his bed and Andrew flashed the light in the lock's direction. Burke opened the case and pulled out an AR-15 and handed it to Andrew.

"Standard 5.56mm," Burke explained, handing Andrew several fully loaded 30-round magazines. "Not much punch so keep it firing."

Andrew slammed a magazine into the rifle and pulled the charger. The lead bullet slammed home with a satisfying metallic thud. He put the rifle to his shoulder and activated the green laser sight that pieced the partial darkness.

Burke nodded and pulled another rifle and several magazines from the case. Andrew gestured toward the rifle and Burke replied, ".458 SOCOM."

"That'll do it," Andrew muttered.

"It better."

Burke took the flashlight from Andrew and the two quickly made their way to the control tent. Burke flipped the light switch upon entering to find the electricity in that tent dead as well.

"All the power must be…" Andrew began.

"The electric fence is down," Burke hissed. "But how'd the mantis…?"

Burke stopped mid-sentence and went to the main radio console then remembering it was electric grabbed one of the hand radios from the charging station and turned it on.

"This is base camp. Eric, are you there? Over."

Static.

Burke tried again.

"Eric. This is base camp. Come in, over."

Nothing.

"Eric! This is base camp! Come in!"

"Maybe their power's out too," Andrew mused.

"Doubtful…"

Andrew looked up from the radio to see Champe and Scarlett entering the tent. Both were fully dressed and Champe was carrying his double rifle and wearing a fully outfitted ammo belt.

"I told you to stay…"

"What's going on?" Champe interrupted. "Why's the power out? And where'd the mantis come from? You said there wouldn't be any in the hunt area. That they were too dangerous."

28.

Eric awoke to agonizing pain.

He looked around then remembered that he was trapped outside the airlock and had no way to escape the narrow ledge he sat upon. The blood on his face and jacket had dried stiff and his arm throbbed in immense pain. His nose was broken, his lip split, and his face heavily bruised. He forced himself to stand then walked to the edge of the ledge. He looked about as if hoping that something had changed during his brief nap but nothing had.

The lab was in darkness, the hunt area thousands upon thousands of feet above him, and the laboratory floor at least half that distance below. He was stranded on the ledge and there was no way off. His only hope was to somehow wait it out until Monday when Alex would hopefully show up for work.

Unless that woman had gotten to him as well.

Beat the crap out of him with a metal rod.

Eric tried to put such thoughts of hopelessness out of mind and scanned the gloom of the lab for anything that might be of help or give him hope. He saw nothing.

But he did hear something.

Something far off in the distance.

Thumping.

A heavy beating sound, reminiscent of helicopter blades churning.

What was it?

The sound grew louder.

And louder.

And louder.

The source came into view and Eric stared at it in disbelief.

It was a housefly. One unlike any he'd ever seen. It was the size of a bull and barreling toward him at incredible speed.

Eric turned and banged on the airlock door in frenzied panic. The fly pounced upon him, slamming his body into the lock and felling him to the ground. Eric fought to get out from under the fly but he was crushed by its immense weight. He screamed in pain and in wild fear. He felt the fly's heavy regurgitated droplet cascade over his back and knew immediately that he was being digested. The liquid stew of acidic enzymes burned through his clothes and into his skin and dissolved into his muscle and toward his skeleton. Eric screamed at the pain and the realization that his demise was mere seconds away. The fly extended its sponging mouthparts and began slurping the syrupy congealment that once was Eric's outer body.

Eric screamed once more then gave into death as his lungs and heart dissolved into liquid.

29.

Burke dropped the radio on the table and cursed.

"What's going on?" Scarlett almost cried. "Where's Bert?"

"Dead," Burke shot back. "He's dead."

Scarlett burst into tears and Champe took her into his arms.

"No power. No communication. The mantis...what the hell is going on?" Burke mused.

Andrew boiled in anger. His friend had just been killed, the camp had fallen into partial ruins, and there appeared to be no escape. Things like this didn't happen by accident.

This was planned.

Planned and executed.

Andrew grabbed Scarlett by the shoulder and spun her around. She stared at him through tear-pooled eyes in shock. Champe started to protest but Andrew cut him off.

"It's you!" Andrew accused. "This is because of you!"

"Andrew!" Burke protested. "What the...?"

"Your husband," Andrew continued. "I'm guessing he found out about you and your boy toy here..."

"Hey!" Champe exploded.

"... And he's cleaning house! Gonna get rid of his cheating wife!" Andrew angrily theorized. "Tell me I'm wrong!"

"Husband!" Burke exploded at Scarlett. "Who's your husband?"

"David Braxton," Andrew explained.

Scarlett fell into heavy sobs and buried her head in Champe's chest. Andrew steamed and anger stormed in Burke's face.

"Braxton's your husband!" Burke spit.

Champe addressed Burke with a nod of affirmation.

Scarlett mumbled through sobs and from the safety of Champe's chest that she was sorry.

"Great!" Burke huffed.

"We don't know…" Champe theorized.

"Cut the shit!" Andrew attacked Champe. "You work for him. You know his reputation. The rumors."

Burke looked to Andrew for explanation.

"Braxton's gotta reputation as a man that takes care of his business. He doesn't let people get in his way." Andrew stared in Scarlett's direction. "Or make him look the fool."

"Is this true?" Burke asked Champe.

Champe separated himself from Scarlett's sobbing form. "He's got that rep. Yes. That's why we've been so careful…"

"Not careful enough," Andrew reasoned. "I'm guessing he found out about you two, cut our power, and released at least one man killer into the mix. That sound about right?"

Scarlett wiped the tears from her eyes and nodded. "He'd do that. He would. Have it done. If he found out about us. About me and Champe. He'd totally do that."

"How lucky for Bert, me, and Burke that we get to experience the fun!" Andrew chided.

Burke fumed in thought. He ran his head through what had happened and what he theorized was happening.

"Here's how we get out of this," Burke began.

30.

Burke laid out his thoughts and his plan.

Braxton wouldn't cut the power and leave them stranded then put in only one mantis. He probably dropped in lots of bugs to better the odds of an "accident" wiping out all of them. There was no way to undo that and no way to get out of the hunt area. The only hope was to make it until Monday morning. Alex would be back then and seeing that they hadn't been extracted from the safari, pull them out.

"What if Alex isn't coming back?" Andrew theorized. "What if no one's coming back?"

"No, Alex will be back," Burke countered. "Braxton would need someone to discover that something went wrong…"

"He can't cash in on my insurance policy without proof of my death," Scarlett grimly interrupted. "If that's what this is all about."

"Your husband's a billionaire," Andrew scoffed. "He's not killing you for insurance money. He's killing you because you're an adulteress! Because you're making him look stupid!"

"That's enough," Champe threatened. "Crap like that doesn't help anyone."

Andrew nodded in agreement and Burke continued.

"Again, all we have to do is make it until Monday."

"There's no way out of the hunt area? You're sure of that?" Champe asked, hoping for a new answer.

"I'm sure. We're in here and at this size until Monday," Burke promised.

Burke continued his plan by explaining that the group had plenty of food and water, a cache of arms, and an abundance of ammo. They had plenty of fuel for the truck and more than enough gas for the lanterns. The climate wasn't an issue even with the power being disabled. It would get hotter than normal but nothing that they couldn't survive.

The biggest hurdle to survival was obviously the insects. Several ants and a rhinoceros beetle had been placed into the area prior to the hunt. God only knew what else had been thrown in the area with them.

Or how many.

All of these would be attracted to the decaying bodies of Bert and the mantis and with the electric fence down, there was nothing to keep them from entering the campsite.

"We're moving to the guest tent. All of us," Burke instructed. "It's elevated and gives us a better defensive position. We'll move everything we need up there. Food, guns, ammo, everything. It'll be tight with the four of us but we'll have to make it work."

"Also some firewood and the grill," Andrew added. "There's enough open space around the tent to have a cook fire. As long as someone's up top keeping watch."

"There's a propane grill out behind the kitchen," Burke detailed. "We can cook on that. Let's keep the firewood for perimeter fires."

Andrew agreed and Champe and Scarlett nodded.

"Sun'll be up soon," Burke declared. "Y'all start carrying things up to the tent. Stay together, stay armed, and be on constant lookout."

"Where are you going?" Andrew asked.

"I'm gonna go block the gate with the truck. Might at least keep the ants and the beetle from getting into camp."

31.

Burke returned to his tent and finished dressing. He pulled on a tactical vest and loaded it with several fully loaded magazines of .458 SOCOM. He took a 1911 .45 caliber pistol from the same tactical case he'd gotten the rifles from and put it on his belt along with two extra clips. He swung the AR-15 over his shoulder and headed to the truck.

The sky above was now void of stars and the faintest beginnings of dawn were starting to show. Burke got into the damaged truck placed his rifle in the driver's seat and started the engine. He turned on all front lights and drove toward the gate. On a whim, Burke tried the truck radio.

"Eric, this is base camp."

Silence.

"Eric, come in."

Silence.

Burke threw the hand mic aside in disgust and watched the road before him. The road was bathed in the brightness of the LEDs and cast long shadows on the larger rocks before him. The gate came into view and Burke cursed what he saw behind it.

"Son of a bitch!"

A bullet ant had somehow managed to get through the exterior gate and was now pushing the one closest to camp off its hinges. Burke gunned the truck and rammed into the gate and the ant behind it. The gate broke from its hinges and the lock that held it and crashed down onto the ant. The truck slammed to a halt and the engine died. Burke cranked the ignition and the truck roared back to life just as the ant recovered from being knocked to the ground. It lay on its back, its legs thrashing at through the fence. Burke downshifted and drove the truck forward and onto the gate. The weight of the truck drove the gate down and further pinned the ant. Burke continued forward until the vehicle was over the ant's abdomen. The beast's chitin armor gave way to the weight and pressure of the truck and exploded in a flood of hemolymph and intestine, glands and stomach. Burke edged the truck forward and the process of explosion repeated twice more as he drove over the giant's thorax then head.

Burke drove to the second gate to find it sheared off from its frame and lying bent and twisted on the ground. He cursed once more then parked the vehicle parallel to the fence in the spot where the gate once was, thinking that a vehicle barrier was better than nothing. He then grabbed his rifle from the front seat and began walking back to camp.

32.

Andrew and Champe were lugging a tactical case up the stairs to the guest tent when Burke returned to camp. He followed them up and into the main part of the tent. The bed and most of the furniture had been pushed aside to make room for several tactical cases, stores of food, two ice chests, and the radios from the command tent.

"You're right," Scarlett announced from her seated position next to a crate of dry goods. She stood and looked over the yellow legal pad in her hand. "We have plenty of food. Enough to last more than a week."

"We only need to hold out for two nights," Burke assured her. "Alex will be in the in the lab Monday morning early, if not sooner."

"You block the gate?" Champe asked, taking a seat on the case he'd just helped carry into the tent.

"Gates are down," Burke began. "Bullet ant rammed through both of them before I could take him out with the truck."

Heavy unease and fear grew on Scarlett's face. Andrew shook his head in depressive realization.

"I parked the truck as a barrier," Burke continued.

"Will that do anything? Realistically?" Champe interrupted.

"It'll slow down the ants. Might keep out the rhino beetle. It'll be just a bump in the road to a mantis though," Burke explained. "Again, we don't know what else is out there."

Burke continued scanning the room, making a mental note of what had already been brought into the tent.

"Looks like y'all just about got everything," Burke announced. "Let's make another sweep of the tents down below, make sure we've got everything we could possibly need then set up a target."

"A target?" Champe scoffed. "For what?"

"So Mrs. Braxton here can learn how to shoot."

33.

"That's twelve o'clock," Burke explained, pointing straight off the porch toward the jungle before them. Andrew, Champe, and Scarlett nodded at the direction and continued listening intently. "The gate's at eleven o'clock, 125 yards out. The dead mantis is back behind us at seven. Most anything that comes into camp is gonna come through that gate and toward the free meal down there in the center of camp. We've got a high wall circling us behind. An electric fence that's not electrified half circling us in front. Andrew and I will watch the front. Champe, you and Scarlett keep watch at our rear."

Andrew, Champe, and Scarlett nodded again then watched as Burke pulled a Barrett Model 82 from the Pelican case next to him.

"Holy shit!" Champe whistled.

"What is that?" Scarlett asked.

"This is what I'll use to take care of anything coming through the gate," Burke explained.

"It's a .50," Champe interrupted.

"Only problem is that we've only got 35 rounds of ammo for it," Andrew explained.

"35 and two tracer rounds," Burke corrected. He pulled down the bipod from the massive rifle and leaned it against the railing of the porch. "I've also got an AR .458 SOCOM and my double rifle."

"And that pistol," Champe pointed out.

Burke ignored the comment and continued.

"Andrew's got his AR-15 and several mags of ammo. Champe's got his double rifle..."

"And 60 rounds of ammo," Champe interrupted once more.

Burke nodded and handed Champe an AR-15.

"You've got this too," Burke continued. "Plus two-30 round mags."

Champe took the rifle, said, "5.56mm. Good," and slammed one of the magazines into the receiver.

Burke opened another Pelican case and took from it a Remington Model 870 tactical shotgun and handed it to Scarlett.

"Come on," Burke instructed.

Scarlett walked to the front railing then listened intently as Burke ran her through the ins and outs of the weapon. Champe tried to offer assistance but was quickly shut down by a stern look from Burke. Once Scarlett assured Burke she understood everything she'd been instructed upon, he pointed to an empty crate on the ground below the tent.

"That's 20 yards out," Burke explained. "Aim dead center. Pull the trigger, jack another round in, then hit it again. Got it?"

Scarlett nodded in the affirmative then shouldered the firearm and shot. The blast knocked her small frame backward and she fought to keep her footing.

"Hit it again!" Burke commanded.

Scarlett stepped forward and fired once more only to stumble slightly backward again. Burke looked down at the buckshot-ravaged box and smiled.

"Good job, Mrs. Braxton," Burke congratulated. "Don't use that unless whatever you're shooting at is up close and personal. To be honest, I'm not sure how well it'll work against bugs as we've never tried it. The shotgun, like all the other weapons here in camp, are mainly used for entertainment purposes. For clients that have never shot 'em before or want to."

"Please call me Scarlett," Scarlett instructed through a stern jaw. "I don't need to be reminded of my husband right now."

"You not being reminded of your husband is what got us into this mess," Burke almost spit. Scarlett's demand had reminded Burke of the anger he'd developed toward her and her careless actions. "And cost the life of a good man. His name was Bert lest you forgot."

Scarlett scowled in anger. Champe saw this and stepped forward to confront Burke.

Burke held up his hand. "Another step forward will be your last step before unconsciousness. I can promise you that."

Andrew exploded forward to put himself in between Burke and Champe.

"Let it go, Champe," Andrew warned. "We need to work together. Like you said earlier."

Champe nodded and turned around. Scarlett tried to catch his eye but he ignored her. He took a deep breath and exhaled then turned back toward Burke.

"Are these all the weapons we have?" Champe changed the subject.

Burke smirked and said, "Other than knives? Yeah. That's all we got."

34.

Burke was halfway down his cigar and the sun at its highest point when he spotted movement just outside the gate. He raised his pair of Swarovski binoculars to his face and studied the grass forest on the other side of the fence. He quickly found a set of bulbous eyes staring in the direction of the Toyota he'd left as a barricade. Burke called to Andrew who quickly came from the side porch of the tent.

"Mantis," Burke announced.

"Shit," Andrew scoffed. "I was hoping the one was...ya know...the only one."

"Wishful thinking on your part," Burke imparted. "I think Braxton's the kinda guy that will give it his all. Not take any chances. Tell the others I'm about to shoot."

Andrew nodded and made his way through the tent to the back porch.

Burk lowered his binoculars and placed them on the table beside him. He picked up the 32-pound monster Barrett rifle and dropped the bipod on the porch railing. He was easing into the rifle when Andrew returned with Champe and Scarlett in tow. Champe had his AR slung to his shoulder and Scarlett held her shotgun at her side. Andrew had his camera on his shoulder and said, "Give me a sec."

"For what?" Burke barked.

"I'm gonna film the shot," Andrew explained. "I'm still on the clock to make a video and that's what I'm gonna do."

Burke shook his head then stared through the scope. He found the mantis and placed the crosshairs on its head. The mantis edged forward and out of the forest and toward the gate. Burke followed it, keeping the crosshair centered on its head.

Champe picked up Burke's binoculars and trained them on the mantis. It was emerald green in color and despite its enormous size moved with cat-like ease and grace. It sulked toward the gate, mindful of every step, its raptorial legs held high and at the ready. It reached the truck then paused as if searching for the best way to climb over the structure.

Burke exhaled slowly and squeezed the trigger. The rifle boomed and the heavy percussion fanned Scarlett's blonde hair outward and back and she clapped her ears in pain from the sound. The 750-grain A-Max bullet slammed into the mantis at 2,820 feet per second and with such force that its head was split in half. Burke jacked another round into the rifle and the spent shell casing fell to the floor and danced in a metallic symphony of bouncing brass. The towering mantis fell forward and onto the truck.

"Another one!" Champe yelled out from behind the binoculars.

Burke scanned the road behind the gate with the Barrett's Vortex Viper scope and quickly found a second mantis. It was tan in color and smaller than the first. It launched from the thorn trees and came to land atop the body of the downed mantis. It plunged its mouth parts into the fallen insect's split head and feasted.

"Disgusting," Champe commented from behind the binoculars he held to his face.

"That's what they eat first," Burke offered. He centered the rifle's crosshairs on feeding beast's head and squeezed the trigger. The rifle thundered and the top section of the mantis' head exploded outward and splattered the road behind it. Burke jacked another round into the .50 and offered, "Two down."

35.

Burke stood and leaned the smoking Barrett against the railing then grabbed a beer from the ice chest. He downed half of it in one swig then looked to Champe and Scarlett.

"Y'all are supposed to be watching our rear," Burke stated.

Champe nodded in agreement, placed the binoculars back on the table, and led Scarlett through the tent toward the stair landing.

Burke relit his cigar and took a seat. Andrew took a seat in the adjoining chair and placed the video camera at his feet.

"Two's probably just the start, isn't it?" Andrew theorized.

"Probably a good guess," Burke countered. He puffed his cigar then took another long pull on his beer. "Braxton's lab boys keep over twenty species of insects in the lab. And we have no idea how many of those he tossed in here with us. Like I said, Braxton's not the kind of guy that does anything half-assed. I'm sure he tossed in more than enough insects to ensure we don't return."

Andrew grabbed a beer from the cooler and sat back down.

"Damn bitch," Burke said before killing his beer. "She got an itch that her old man couldn't satisfy and we all suffer the consequences."

Andrew took a long drink on his then offered, "True. But I suggest we worry about that once we get out of here. Best case scenario, we've got...what? 36 hours give or take before Alex comes in?"

"Let's hope so," Burke offered.

36.

"I can't believe you didn't take up for me," Scarlett scowled from her seat on the porch.

Champe ignored the comment and kept his gaze on the thick jungle that stood between him and the barrier walls of the hunt area.

"I mean, really!" Scarlett continued.

Champe turned to face Scarlett.

"Really, what?" Champe countered. "Andrew was right. We need to work together. We're in a shit storm here that we may never get out of. Do you get that?"

Scarlett lowered her head and mumbled that she did. She wiped the welling tears from her eyes then looked back to Champe.

"I'm scared," she whined. "Really scared."

Champe felt no compassion for Scarlett at that moment. Rather, he felt disgust. Disgust at himself for falling for her charms, her attractiveness, wealth, youth, and incredible sexual desire. He was pissed that he'd allowed himself to go down this path. The best that could happen to him was getting out of the hunt area alive but with no job or potential career to speak of. The worst that could happen would be being eaten alive by something he could have easily stepped on only a few days earlier. He had a great life and an even better future ahead of him. Regardless of what happened in the next day and a half, all of that was gone. His predicament was just as much his fault as hers. Maybe if he could get Scarlett out of the area alive, they could prove her husband tried to have them killed. If so, maybe he could sue him. At least get enough money out of that situation to jump-start his life into a new career.

That became his new goal.

Survival at any cost so he could sue that son of a bitch.

Champe swallowed his newly realized feelings for Scarlett and his plan at hand and explained, "You're doing great. And we'll get out of this no problem. I promise you."

Scarlett smiled and stood and took Champe into her arms. She kissed him and cooed, "You better be right 'cause I'm looking forward to lots more fun with you. Lots more."

Champe suppressed his sudden sexual desires and assured Scarlett that he looked forward to their upcoming time together as well.

37.

Alex rolled out of bed and made his way to the bathroom. He relieved himself then downed the lukewarm Dr. Pepper he'd left next to the sink the day before.

Or maybe it was two days before.

No matter.

He drank it in one long pull then headed to the refrigerator to grab a fresh soda. He downed half of that then made his way to the couch. He opened the pizza box on the coffee table before him and took a slice of pineapple, mushroom, sausage, and pepperoni and shoved it into his mouth. He cranked on his TV and gaming system and put on his headphones and adjusted his microphone. He signed onto his account, pulled up his elf avatar, then checked out who he'd be exploring the medieval world with. It appeared as though all his usual friends were already logged in and one of them called over the game system to give him a hard time about bailing out of the game so early the night before.

"Did Alex Reyxidor the Magnificent get his beauty rest?" one voice joked.

"'Cause we know he didn't have a date," another voice joked.

"Got some much-needed sleep and am ready for a 20-hour-minimum adventure," Alex blasted back.

He ran his eyes over the list of participants then caught that Eric was logged on but hadn't done anything since early last night.

"Is Eric on?" Alex asked.

"Screw him!" a voice blasted over the system. "He bailed last night with no notice, leaving me to fight off a cave dragon with nothing but my dick in my hand."

"You always have your dick in your hand," another voice countered.

Alex laughed then picked up his cell phone. He texted Eric, "Where you at? Just got online to find you missing. All okay at lab?" then immersed himself into the fantasy world that he far preferred over real life.

38.

Andrew turned the four steaks on the grill then closed the lid and looked up to see Burke keeping watch.

"About five minutes," Andrew relayed to Burke.

"Medium rare," Burke called down to Andrew. "Lots of pink. Don't screw it up."

"Let me worry about the steaks," Andrew countered. "You just keep an eye out for bugs."

Burke smirked at Andrew then studied the jungle before him. There had been no sign of life since the two mantises almost five hours ago. He expected that would change soon as it'd be getting dark in a few hours. Who knows what would be coming out of the woodwork at that point.

Andrew called that he was coming up with the steaks. Burke nodded, slung his AR-15 .458 SOCOM over his shoulder, and headed through the tent to the landing where Champe and Scarlett were keeping guard.

"Andrew's coming up with the steaks," Burke announced. "Y'all take a break. Enjoy your meal. Andrew will keep watch back here."

"You sure?" Champe asked.

Burke nodded. "Sure. Take your time. We'll need you well rested for tonight."

Champe nodded and Scarlett stepped forward to Burke.

"Thank you," she offered. "I know you think this is my fault and   yet..."
Burke held up his hand for Scarlett to stop but she continued.

"I just wanted to say I appreciate..."

"There's your steaks now," Burke interrupted, pointing to Andrew and the large platter of meat he held before him.

"They look wonderful," Scarlett said, changing gears. "I have no idea why I'm so hungry but I'm famished."

"Good deal," Andrew exclaimed. "All are the same. Medium rare. I hope that's okay."

"That's fabulous," Scarlett said, taking the tray from Andrew.

"Y'all enjoy your meal," Andrew continued. "Burke and I—"

"I already told them to…" Burke paused midsentence. He turned his head toward the front porch where he'd been keeping watch.

"What is…?" Scarlett started.

"Be quiet!" Burke spat.

Burke heard it again, the sound of metal wire pinging under heavy strain. He rushed to the front porch. Andrew, Champe, and Scarlett followed. Burke looked to the gate to see only the truck and two dead mantises. He followed the fence to the right until he came to the source of the strain and the metallic noises.

An emperor scorpion, black as pitch, almost four times the size of an African elephant, fought to free itself from the large horizontal cables of the fence. Burke theorized it had tried climbing through the fence only to get caught. It struggled and spun, twisted and wound itself in the wire trying to free itself. The wire screamed in metallic pitch as it was pulled from the massive fence posts. The scorpion became more entangled and it thrashed violently in effort to free itself.

"We might have a problem," Andrew muttered. He grabbed his camera from the table and zoomed in on the melee at the fence.

"Problem why?" Champe asked.

Champe's question was answered when Burke fired the .50 Barrett at the monstrosity. The 750-grain bullet ricocheted off the scorpion's head with a spark of metal cutting concrete.

"No way," Champe uttered in disbelief. "Did that just… It just bounced off him!"

"We tried hunting them at our current size once before," Andrew explained from behind his camera. "It can't be done…"

"Bullshit it can't be done," Burke barked. He jacked another round into the rifle and fired once more. The bullet sparked off the elephantine beast and it reacted by thrashing in the wire even further.

"We don't have anything that'll go through him," Andrew finished.

"At least he's stuck," Champe offered.

"For now," Scarlett said pessimistically.

Burke fired once more only to watch in disgust as the bullet yet again sparked off the beasts' head.

The scorpion rolled in the wire further and Burke noticed that the truck was tangled in the cables now as well. Every roll of the scorpion's body or pull of its pinchers pulled the truck closer to it. Burke fired again at the scorpion to no avail. The bullet grazed its head, unleashing a heavy spark the color of burnt orange. The truck was dragged along the fence-line like a toy, as were the two mantises that clung to it in death. When the truck was only five feet from the monster arachnoid, Burked trained his rifle on its gas tank and fired. The heavy bullet punched completely through both sides of the vehicle, unleashing a torrent of gas. Burke pulled a tracer round from the ammo case next to him and loaded it into the Barrett and fired. The incendiary round ignited the gas and it and two dead mantises and the scorpion exploded into flames.

Andrew, Champe, and Scarlett cheered.

Burke jacked another round into the rifle then paused to watch the still-writhing scorpion burn.

"It's not...dead," Scarlett offered. "It's not dead! It's still thrashing   about!"

"Let its shell cook for a second," Burke explained. "That'll soften it up."

Burke watched the scorpion burn and fight against the trappings of the cables and the truck that anchored them. After a minute, he trained on the beast's head and fired. The bullet struck home with an explosive force that spread primitive brain and body fluids over a 20-foot spread. Burke fired once more and the area was painted again. The scorpion fell into the flames and burned.

Burke leaned the Barrett against the railing, lit a cigar, and decreed, "Y'all go eat your steak before it gets cold."

39.

Alex was starting to worry.

It had been six hours since he sent Eric his initial text and he'd yet to receive a reply.

None of his texts had received a reply.

Alex tried calling both Eric's cell and two different lines at the lab but had gotten nothing other than voicemail.

This wasn't like Eric.

Not at all.

Eric was anal about signing out of video games and chat rooms, about answering texts, and especially about phone calls. Sure, he could be forgetful. He was always losing his keys. But he was always in the know and responsive where messages were concerned.

Alex pondered all of this until he got a call over the game system from one of the elves in his clan. He returned to the game with fervor and put Eric out of his mind.

40.

Andrew and Champe dumped their last load of logs onto the pile that sat some 100 yards from the porch that Burke kept watch from. Andrew poured a healthy amount of kerosene onto the pile, lit a match, and tossed it onto the stack. The kerosene ignited in a flash and the bonfire flamed to life. He and Champe walked back toward the high tent, pausing only long enough to light the lanterns that had been moved to encircle the tent that now served as the group's last stand.

They climbed the stairs and walked to where Burke sat. Scarlett followed them.

"Everything's lit," Andrew reported. "If anything comes our way, we'll be sure to see it."

"Good," Burke mumbled. "Everybody got their flashlights? Weapons?"

"Locked and loaded," Champe said, holding aloft his AR.

Scarlett nodded and gestured to the shotgun she held at her side, and Andrew unslung his AR and held it before him.

"We should try to rotate throughout the night in shifts," Burke explained. He looked to Andrew and Scarlett. "Why don't you two get some shut-eye. Andrew and I will take first watch."

"I'm too up to sleep," Scarlett explained. "I'd just be wasting time if I lay down."

"Me too," Champe insisted. "I'm good to go."

"Y'all's call," Burke explained. "Just don't feel that you have to stay awake."

Champe and Scarlett said that they genuinely wanted to stay up and stand guard. Not only that, but they felt it was their duty.

Burke said he understood and told them again not to feel obligated to do so. Scarlett excused herself from the party and told Champe she'd meet him on the stair landing after a quick trip to the bathroom.

She went to the bathroom and checked herself in the mirror. She washed her face with cold water, brushed her teeth, and reapplied her lipstick then headed to the landing with the shotgun cradled in her arms. Champe wasn't on the landing but she could hear the faint echo of his voice from the opposite side of the tent. He was apparently still talking to Burke.

Scarlett scanned the grounds before her making note of how beautiful that section of the camp looked painted in the amber colorings of lantern light. She looked to the two burnt sections where Burke's and Bert's tents had once stood then turned away to put thoughts of what had transpired there out of her mind. Her thoughts ran to the outburst from Burke and Andrew concerning her affair with Champe as the explanation for the group's current predicament. She accepted that they were correct.

She knew that cheating on her husband was wrong.

But he had all but ignored her since their marriage.

He never wanted to go out or to do anything.

He didn't appreciate all the time she took to keep herself attractive, to keep up with his social engagements, or being his rock during difficult times.

And he never wanted to have sex.

Not ever.

Which was something she just didn't understand because almost everybody that saw her wanted to have sex with her.

And so when Champe flirted with her at a party, she jumped on him, figuratively and literally.

Scarlett's thoughts were interrupted by something about a foot and a half off the railing before her. She walked toward it and tilted her head this way and that way, trying to understand what the long vertical mirror of light was. The object was thin, about the diameter of a garden hose, and translucent. Light bounced off of it in a strange manner and she couldn't identify what it was no matter how hard she tried.

She knew in the back of her mind that she shouldn't touch it but it was too beautiful not to. She had to know what it was. It was just so gorgeous the way the light shined through and off of it. She took the shotgun into her left hand and reached beyond the railing with her right. The mirrored rope was further out than she thought and she had to stand on her tiptoes in order to stretch out to reach it.

It was cold.

Semi-wet.

And sticky.

She jerked her hand back in sudden fright but the rope was stuck to her fingers. She pulled back even further and the rope jerked her forward and over the railing. She dropped the shotgun and instinctively reached for the rope with her left hand so as not to fall. That hand too became stuck and she swung to and fro as she struggled to free herself. Her head was flung back in the action and she saw above her hundreds if not thousands of translucent ropes shimmering in the starlight, crossing and crisscrossing one another, and she realized that she was caught in a web. She tried to scream but fright stole her voice, replacing it instead with only gasps for air.

The dark form of a cribellate orb weaver spider eased from the darkness above her and onto the rope that held her prisoner.

Scarlett struggled to scream, struggled to free herself but she could do neither. The bear-sized spider daintily climbed down its thread and took Scarlett into its massive front arms. The nightmare spun the girl before it, wrapping her in an ever-tightening noose of silk. Scarlett wept at the pain and in fear as the silk tightened around her legs. The pressure built and the bones snapped inward and broke. Her hips were crushed and her lower ribs caved. She fought to breathe then gave way to the darkness that washed over her.

41.

Champe exited the tent and into a living nightmare.

His mind could barely comprehend the events unfolding before him.

Scarlett was being cocooned by a spider the size of a grizzly. Champe watched as her dead eyes stared forward into nothingness as her body turned on a spit only to be wrapped in translucent steel cables.

Champe screamed in horror and disbelief. He raised his AR-15 and fired and as fast as his finger could master the semiautomatic rifle. The cribellate orb weaver danced and gyrated as its body was pockmarked by bullets. It sprang from its perch above Scarlett's now completely enshrined body and onto Champe.

Champe was knocked to the porch floor. The rifle flew from his hands. The spider pressed down on Champe and opened its mouthparts. Champe strained to push the beast off of him. He called on all his might and pushed its head upward and away from his face then watched in horror as fluid pooled in its mouth. Burke and Andrew ran onto the porch. Andrew rushed forward and raised his rifle to the spider's head. Burke yelled, "NO!" just as Andrew fired. The bullet punched through the spider's lower head, unleashing a torrent of fluids. Champe turned his head just as the beast exploded above him. He felt the warm burn of the spider's digestive juices as they poured onto his ear and neck. Burke dropped his rifle and reached under the spider's body.

"Help!" Burke commanded Andrew.

Andrew dropped his rifle and joined Burke and together they rolled the dead spider off Champe, off the porch, and onto the ground below. Champe scrambled to his feet and grabbed his ear in pain. Burke pulled the disoriented hunter by the arm and dragged him to the bathroom and threw him into the shower. He turned the handle and thrust Champe under the running water.

"It's digestive juices. Like acid," Burke hurriedly explained. "Get it off of you!"

Champe starred at Burke in confusion. The shock of all that had happened in less than the span of two minutes flooded his body with adrenaline and fear and he felt sick. His mind raced ahead for answers. He blurted out, "Scarlett!" and tried to exit the shower. Burke pushed him back under the water and said, "She's gone!"

"What? No!"

"She's gone. There's nothing we can do. She's gone."

Champe dropped to the shower floor and retched.

42.

Andrew was staring at the suspended cocoon that held Scarlett's body when Burke returned to the porch.

"I didn't know about the acid vomit...whatever the hell that was," Andrew began. "I wouldn't have fired had I known. You know that... Is he gonna be okay?"

Burke took a cigar from his shirt pocket and put it in his mouth. He chewed on it for a second then nodded. "He'll be fine. It works slow. We got it off in time."

"We didn't get to her in time," Andrew said, returning his gaze toward the wrapping that contained Scarlett's body.

Burke ignored the comment and returned to the inside of the tent. He grabbed a ceremonial spear that was used as decoration and tied his sheath knife to the end of the long wooden handle. He returned to the porch and began sawing the webbing that held Scarlett aloft.

"She'll drop to the ground," Andrew cautioned.

"Don't think it matters at this point," Burke said as he continued his sawing.

The blade cut halfway through the tightrope and Scarlett's bodyweight did the rest. Her body fell to the ground below, landing next to the spider that had killed her.

Andrew grabbed a blanket from inside the tent and ventured down the stairs and covered her body. He returned topside just as Champe walked onto the porch. Champe saw what Andrew did and he thanked him.

"I'm afraid that's the best we can do," Burke offered. "That webbing is used to constrict the prey's body..."

"I understand," Champe said, ending the explanation. He had seen the webbing work its magic. The last thing he wanted was to relive the situation with scientific explanation.

"I'm sorry," Andrew offered.

Champe nodded in gratitude and winced in pain.

"What's wrong?" Burke asked. "You hurt?"

"Think I broke my collarbone," Champe explained. "My left side."

"Can you still shoot?" Burke asked.

"Don't think I have much choice," Champe explained.

"You don't," Burke instructed. He handed Champe his AR-15. "Not if you want to live."

43.

Alex's coffee table was a wasteland of empty soda cans, discarded tortilla chip bags, pizza crust, and candy wrappers. He had been playing online for going on 14 hours and his eyes and face showed the strain. He stood from the couch and made his way to the kitchen. He searched the refrigerator and cabinets for something to eat but found nothing but more empty vessels and a few canned goods he didn't remember purchasing. He returned to the couch and picked up his cell phone.

There was still no reply from Eric.

That was odd.

Very odd.

Eric never went this long without responding to texts.

Especially when he was in the lab.

Alex decided to go to the lab to see what was going on for himself.

44.

Champe was fuming.

His feelings had moved from disbelief to fear to the acceptance of Scarlett's killing to raging anger.

"He's gonna pay for this!" Champe said to himself as much as to Burke. "I swear to God, Braxton's gonna pay for this. For Scarlett... Bert..."

"Let's worry about survival for now," Burke exclaimed. "Let's focus on that."

Champe clinched his jaw and stared off the porch and toward the darkness that lie beyond the lanterns and the still-burning bonfire. He could make out a few glowing ambers that sat smoldering near the truck fire but beyond that was an abyss of black. The stars and half-moon above offered some light but none permeated the tall grass forest and whatever lurked within it.

Burke let Champe fume and walked through the tent to the stair landing where Andrew stood guard.

"All clear?" Burke asked.

Andrew turned and said, "Nothing. Although...morbid as it sounds, I'm sure something will soon enough smell..."

Burke nodded that he understood that Andrew was referring to Scarlett and the spider.

"How's he doing?" Andrew asked.

"Looks like first-degree, maybe second-degree burns on his ear and neck. Not much worse than a sunburn. Broken collarbone's causing him trouble. I'm worried about him being able to shoot..."

"About Scarlett," Andrew corrected. "I was talking about how's he doing with her loss. Can't be easy watching somebody you'd been intimate with…"

"Intimate?" Burke chuckled. "Ya mean screwing?"

Andrew laughed. "Damn but if you ain't a hard ass. Is it all the killing that makes you so stoic?"

"Nope," Burked assured Andrew. "It's all the people I interact with."

Andrew continued laughing. "Okay. I'll agree with you on that one. Nothing can make you lose faith in humanity quite like humanity."

"You can say that again," Burke agreed, smiling.

The two men continued laughing for a time then fell into a period of silence. Burke lit the cigar he'd been chewing on then grabbed two beers from the ice chest just inside the tent. He popped the top on one and handed it to Andrew. Burke popped the second beer then clinked his bottle against Andrew's and said, "Here's to lost faith in humanity."

The men drank for a time then Burke said, "Keep the watch," and entered the tent. He fished another beer from the cooler and walked back toward the porch where he'd left Champe. Burke handed Champe the fresh beer and he nodded in thanks then took a long pull.

"That's good," Champe offered. "Thanks again."

"You need anything for the pain?" Burke asked. "We've got a couple different painkillers in the med kit."

Champe took another pull on his beer then said, "I'll take a look in a few. It's not so bad right now."

Burke ignored Champe's response and instead walked to the railing. He stared into the darkness to just beyond the bonfire. There, in the dancing shadows of the flames, he saw something.

Something moving.

But what?

Burke killed his beer and tossed the bottle aside. He grabbed the Barrett .50 and dropped its tripod on the railing. He eased into the rifle and stared through the scope.

"What?" Champe whispered. He scanned the darkness, trying to see what Burke was aimed on. "I don't see anything."

The flames of the bonfire were sucked back then fanned upward to three times their height as a mantis flew from the darkness and over the fire. Burke fired the massive cannon. The bullet overshot the insect in flight and sparked in impact at the stones it hit instead. Burke fired once more and this time the bullet hit home, striking the mantis just behind its head. The monstrous insect tumbled from flight and into the earth below. Burke fired a third time. The bullet pierced the beast's head, nearly splitting its head in two. Burke fired one final shot and the insect's head disintegrated into a fine mist of hemolymph, brain, and eyes.

45.

Andrew rushed through the tent and to the porch. He arrived just in time to see Burke's final shot destroy the mantis' head. Champe was holding his shoulder in pain, the apparent victim of massive blowback from the Barrett's firing. Burke stood and leaned the smoking rifle against the railing. The tent and the platform it stood upon suddenly lurched forward and the Barrett fell to the floor. Burke grabbed his AR-15 and looked to Andrew then Champe.

"Earthquake?" Champe asked. "How's that possible...?"

The tent dropped an inch and the three men fell to the floor. They scrambled to their feet in haste then fell again as the floor shot forward then back again.

"What the hell?!" Andrew questioned in anger as he fought his way back to his feet.

The back end of the platform collapsed and the three men slid downward in the direction of the stair landing. Burke grabbed the bathroom doorframe on the way down and jerked to a halt. Champe rolled to the side and grabbed the outer railing. He screamed in agonizing pain at the impact of his broken collarbone against railing's support pole but managed to grab tight and keep from sliding further. Burke and Champe watched as Andrew slid downward and toward the ground. The earth opened in an explosion of rock and stone. Two massive paddles, each the size of a small car and covered in rows of long black spikes, parted the churned soil and pulled into view a head constructed of nightmares. The beast caught sight of Andrew's descending body and reached upward and pinned him to the floor with the spikes of his paddle. Andrew howled in pain then in panic as he was pulled downward and toward the mole cricket's opening mouthparts. Burke pulled himself upward and straddled the doorframe. He raised his AR and trained on the insect's head. The lower half of Andrew's body disappeared into the monster's primitive jaws. Andrew released a primitive cry as his body was halved. The beast pulled the remainder of Andrew's body into its mouth. Burke changed his aim and put a .458 SOCOM through Andrew's head. The elephantine cricket slurped Andrew's body into its mouth and trained its sight on Champe struggling for dear life only 15 feet above him.

The tent platform jerked and shook as a second mole cricket burrowed from the earth next to the first. It slammed its spiked paddle into the floor and began climbing upward and toward Champe.

Burke swung his AR toward the second monster and fired. The cricket shook its head at the impact of the 300-grain bullet against its snout and continued its climb. Burked fired again and again. Bullet after bullet slammed into the burrowing demon's head, punching through chitin armor, making pulp of its insides. The cricket succumbed to death and slid downward and into the first cricket's grasp. It pulled the partially destroyed insect into its mouthparts and began feeding.

"The Barrett!" Burke called down to Champe. "Can you reach it?"

Champe sat perched in shock.

"The Barrett!" Burke yelled once more. "Right below you!"

Champe shook himself to and looked about. He saw the Barrett rifle caught by its bipod on the railing two support poles below him. Champe looked beyond it to the monster feeding on its own kind maybe eight feet below the rifle.

"Yes or no?!" Burke demanded.

Champe looked to the rifle then to the feeding frenzy then back up to Burke.

"No," Champe admitted. "I can't."

"Then climb up," Burke instructed.

Champe nodded and pulled himself along the railing and up the 45-degree angle toward the tent platform's highest point. Burke scanned the bathroom looking for weapons. He didn't see any. He shouldered his AR and began his climb out of the tent and toward the top railing.

46.

"What now?!" Champe almost cried in desperation. "We can't stay perched up here for the next few days. What with one rifle and that spawn up from Hell down there…"

"Mole cricket. Nasty buggers," Burke explained. "The sun'll be up soon. It'll burrow down and outta the light and heat beforehand…"

"So we just perch up here like birds on a wire until then?!"

Burke pulled a cigar from his pocket and put it in his mouth. He reached into his pocket for his clipper then clipped the end of the Arturo Fuente and put it back in his mouth. He dropped the clipper in his pocket then spit and said, "I'm open to ideas."

Champe scowled in the half dark.

The beast below continued consuming its meal and Burke lit his cigar.

47.

Alex entered the dark lab and called out for Eric.

No one answered.

Alex flipped the light switch on the wall but no lights came on.

He walked to the desk and turned the knob on the desk lamp.

Nothing.

He ran his finger along the tracking pad of the computer in an attempt to bring it to life.

Nothing.

He fished his cell phone from his pocket and used it as a flashlight.

He saw the radios all open and absent of batteries strewn about the desk.

What was going on?

He turned 180 degrees, flashing his light before him looking for some sort of answer. Something upon the glass door of the shrink chamber caught his eye. He walked toward it, the light of his cell phone illuminating his path.

What was that?

Was that...?

Blood?

The smear ran the downward length of the door.

Alex flashed his light inside the chamber.

He saw drops of blood and blood-smeared handprints.

Fear eased its way up his spine.

His shivered then pulled himself from the view of the chamber.

He moved toward the sealed room where the hunt area was housed.

The hunt area was up near the skylight as it was supposed to be.

But where was Eric?

Alex directed the light from his cell along the wall and to the breaker box for the lab.

All the breakers were off.

He turned them on and the lab slowly came to life.

Lights came on, computers booted up, and air began to circulate.

Alex returned to the shrinking chamber to study the blood under regular light.

He hoped against hope it wasn't Eric's.

Or anyone else that he knew.

Alex returned to the desk that housed the bank of radios. He took one into his hand then started searching drawer after drawer for batteries. He found some rechargeables of the correct size, loaded them into the radio, and held them in place with his hand as he couldn't find the back cover.

48.

Burke puffed his cigar and watched the mole cricket below him feed. It had devoured most of the other cricket and Burke knew it'd be only a matter of time before it would start searching for other food sources. Burke checked his watch then informed Champe that the sun would be up in less than a half hour. Champe nodded and steadied himself above the tilted railing.

A metallic screech suddenly pierced the air, its yowling attracting the attention of the feeding monstrosity below. It sniffed the air and listened for the vibrations associated with the new intruder.

Burke realized the noise was emanating from his radio and he yanked the handheld unit from its pocket on his tactical vest and held it to his face.

"Hello!" Burke called into the radio. "This is Burke. Come in."

The cricket tossed the carcass it had been feeding on aside and drove the spikes of its front flippers into the wooden decking and began pulling itself up. The tent shook and jerked on what was left of its support poles and Burke and Champe struggled to hang tight.

"Burke! This is Alex," the radio screeched. "What's going on? Where's Eric?"

"Shut up and listen!" Burke barked. The tent jumped under the weight of the cricket's climb. "Get us outta here, now!"

Burke handed the radio to Champe and trained his rifle on the ever-approaching mole cricket. It was halfway up the platform and gaining fast. Burke studied himself and fired.

"What's going on?" Alex questioned through static. "Wait? Is that gunfire?"

"Scarlett's dead! Bert is dead…"

"Who are they?" Alex asked. "… Who are you?"

"I'm Champe Carter! Get us out of here now!"

The cricket drove its right flipper into the flooring and the wooden planks gave way. The support pole beneath it snapped and the entire structure collapsed. The mole cricket fell backward and on top of the half-eaten carcass. Burke held onto his rifle and rolled forward upon impact. Champe came to land hard and the railing fell upon his left leg and he felt the bones within it snap. He howled in pain and grabbed his leg. Burke came up from his forward summersault and staggered forward, firing into the gigantic insect as he did. Bullet after bullet slammed home into the beast's head and its body jerked and twisted in response. Burke emptied the rifle's magazine, hit the release, dropped the empty, slammed home a new magazine, and fired four more times. The cricket collapsed dead and Burke fired one last shot into the oozing fountain that once was its alien head. He turned and ran through the rubble and toward Champe.

"The radio!" he demanded. "Where's the radio?!"

Champe writhed in pain and answered through clenched teeth, "I don't know. I dropped…"

Burke scanned the fallen and crushed remains of the five-star accommodations for the radio. The sun had partially risen and although the camp was cast in gray light, shadows and dark spots remained.

"Burke! Burke, come in!"

Burke trained on the radio's call and followed it to its source beneath the split remains of a bedside table.

"Alex," Burke commanded. "This is Burke. I need you to get us outta here as fast as you can. This is beyond an emergency situation. The hunt's been sabotaged…"

"Sabotaged?" Alex looked around the lab in a new understanding.

"How long before you can extract us?'

Alex scanned the lab. He took a quick assessment of the equipment and its status, factored some ideas through his head then explained, "Things were all but shut down up here…"

"I don't give a shit, Alex! Gimme an answer, God dammit!!"

"Uh…" Alex stuttered in speech and thought. "I'm gonna need at least 45 minutes…"

"We don't have that!"

"Maybe a half hour," Alex panicked. "I've got to lower the hunt area, reboot

the…"

"We're on our way to the airlock now," Burke countered. "Make it happen. Burke out!"

49.

Burke shoved the radio back in his vest and called to Champe. "Start digging yourself out. We're leaving."

"My leg's broken," Champe said, wincing.

"Of course it is," Burke muttered to himself in disgust.

"What?"

"Nothing. Do the best you can. I'll be there in a sec."

Morning had come into full view and the sun shown down on the remains of a disaster area. The tent—or what was left of it—was a storm path of broken furniture, smashed bathroom fixtures, food and food containers, and torn and shredded canvas. Burke stepped through the destruction, looking for the tools he'd need to survive until he could exit the area. He found the Barrett rifle but didn't trust the slight warp of its barrel. It had apparently been bent somehow in the collapse. Burke found the shotgun, checked it, and found it fully loaded with six rounds plus one in the chamber. He searched the area around the gun for more shells but found none then remembered that Scarlett had them on her when she was wrapped up tight.

Stupid bitch.

If she had kept her legs closed, none of this would have happened.

Burke dismissed his anger and kept searching for weapons.

There were two more AR-15s somewhere in the rubble.

And two safari rifles as well.

He had to find them.

"Burke!"

Burke turned from his search toward a panic-stricken Champe. He had freed himself from the rubble that had fallen upon him and all but crushed his leg and was crawling over debris and toward him.

50.

Alex logged onto the computer and brought up the systems control.

He initiated the lowering of the hunt area and began cycling through the checklist of controls for powering on the shrinking mechanism. He rebooted the airlock controls and powered up the tram.

"This is gonna take...some time," Alex exhaled in stress. "Too much time."

He felt a sudden flicker on his arm and brought his hand down on it with a heavy slap. He recoiled his hand in disgust at the wetness on his palm and wiped the mush on his pants' leg.

"Freakin' fly!" he complained aloud. He wiped his hand again and exclaimed, "Gross. Who knows what you've been into!"

51.

Burke looked past Champe's crawling form to just beyond the fallen tent to see a striped bark scorpion racing forward. The beast was a blur of light tan and brownish yellow, of flailing pinchers and cold, black, orb-like eyes. It was three times the size of a bull rhino and closing fast.

"Shit!" Burke raised his AR-15 .458 SOCOM and fired. The bullet slammed through the monsters' right eye and into its cephalothorax. It continued forward seemingly unfazed and onto the fallen remains of the tent. Burke fired again. The bullet hit just behind where the creature's eye had been and ricocheted upward. The scorpion reached out and pinched Champe's broken leg in its right pedipalp. Champe screamed in agony. His body was pulled from the floor, his broken leg twisted, and he could feel his leg bones separate further. All that kept him from falling from the scorpion's iron grip was his ever-stretching muscle and loose skin. Burke fired two more times into the behemoth's cephalothorax and it fell forward. The scorpion's pincher constricted in death and Champe's leg was sheared from his body. He fell to the ground and immediately rolled over and took what was left of his leg into his hands. Arterial blood shot through his fingers and pooled on the floor.

Burke reached Champe and dropped to his side. He ignored Champe's screams of agony and reached for the fallen man's belt. He unbuckled it and pulled it from Champe's belt loops. Burke pushed Champe's hands away from his leg and fought to cinch the belt around the leg turned geyser. Burke cinched the belt and

Champe howled in pain. Burke pulled the makeshift tourniquet tighter and Champe screamed even louder.

"Listen!" Burke directed. "Listen to me."

Champe shook in uncontrollable pain. He was pale beyond words. His lips a growing shade of blue and his eyes struggled to focus.

"Listen," Burke commanded. "I can't move you like this…"

Champe shook to life. He grabbed Burke by the shirt with all his might and pulled him down toward him.

"No… You can't… You can't leave me…"

"I can't move you in this condition," Burke continued. "I've got to get help…"

Something suddenly washed over Champe.

His pain eased.

He felt as if he could breathe easier.

He was no longer as scared.

He let go of Burke's shirt and let his hands drop to his side.

Burke took one of Champe's hands and placed it around the belt.

"Keep this tight," Burke instructed. "You understand?"

Whether Champe understood or didn't understand, complied or didn't comply, didn't matter at this point.

Burke knew that.

He knew that Champe would be dead within the hour if not sooner. Champe had suffered too much.

Lost too much blood.

Endured far too much to rebound from.

"I…understand," Champe assured Burke. His voice was soft but sure. "Gimme a gun though."

Burke unslung the shotgun from his shoulder.

Champe shook his head in disagreement and pointed to the 1911 on Burke's belt. Burke gave the dying man his wish by pulling the .45 semiautomatic from its holster and handed it to Champe.

"Seven in the clip and one in the pipe," Burke decreed.

Champe nodded then lowered his head in apparent shame.

"Sorry I got you into this," Champe confessed. "I promise I didn't know that Braxton knew. I knew she was trouble… It was just that… She was so…"

"I know," Burke conceded. "Women always get the better of us…"

Champe smiled.

Burke returned Champe's smile, stood, and left.

52.

Champe heard the ants before he could see them.

But then he knew he wouldn't see them until they were right on top of him.

He couldn't lift his head.

He was too weak.

He felt the suddenly throbbing of the floor beneath him and realized the ants must have walked onto the tent platform.

Or what was left of it.

Champe heard the heavy clicking of their mandibles, the clopping of their claws upon the wooden flooring, and the swishing of their antennae. He pulled his tourniquet tighter and raised the .45.

The lead bullet ant stood over him as if questioning what it had suddenly found. It tilted its head and stared at the food source below it.

It reared its head back.

Opened its mandibles.

And eased down toward Champe.

Champe fired.

The force of the gun slammed his elbow into the ground and Champe fired again.

And again.

He felt the sudden warmth of the liquids showering out of the ant and over his face and neck.

He kept firing.

Until he counted to seven.

He released the tourniquet.

Put the pistol beneath his chin.
And fired one last time.

53.

Burke counted the .45 shots as they were unleashed.

He could tell by the sound that whatever Champe was shooting at was probably right on top of him and he hoped he'd at least made his last bullet count.

Burke reached the outer door that connected the hunt area to the airlock to the tram. He hit the control panel.

Nothing happened.

The door didn't open.

He unslung the shotgun from his shoulder, leaned it against the wall, and pulled his radio.

"Alex!" he barked. "This is Burke. Come in…"

"Almost," the radio answered.

"Almost what?" Burke shot back.

"The doors are almost aligned," Alex explained.

Burke saw the ants in the campground.

He could see at least four of them through the foliage.

"How long, Alex?"

"Maybe 10 minutes…"

"I ain't got 10 minutes!"

Burke slammed the radio into his vest in disgust.

He put his back to the door, slid down into a crouch, and trained his AR on the path before him. The first bullet ant came down the path at a cautionary clip. It was still searching, not entirely sure of Burke's presence. Burke aimed for the brain and fired off two shots. The ant's head jerked back then fell forward and into the earth. No sooner had its body fell than another ant was scurrying over it and toward Burke.

Burke aimed for the brain and fired.

The ant's head jerked to the side and Burke fired again. Burke heard the metallic click of an empty chamber. He cursed the rifle, dropped the magazine, pulled the last .458 SOCOM magazine from his vest, slammed it home, and fired twice more into the ant's brain. The ant fell in front of the first ant's body and sent upward clouds of stone and earth.

The trees to the side of the trail and before the duo of fallen insects parted and a third bullet ant barreled forward. Burke unleashed his final five rounds into the ant and it too collapsed into a shower of earth and debris. Burke tossed the AR aside and put the shotgun to his shoulder just as a fourth ant launched onto the trail. It ran forward with the force of a bull elephant, closing the gap of between it and Burke to 20 yards in a matter of seconds. Burke slam fired four rounds of buckshot in the direction of the ant. The shot bounced off the ant as if it was being pelted with nothing more than snowballs.

Burke continued slam firing the shotgun.

The ant barreled forward until it was almost in Burke's lap.

The door opened behind Burke and he fell backward and onto the tarmac.

The ant thrust its head into the opening. The doors closed inward, trapping the ant's head in place. The beast opened its mandibles. Burke shoved the barrel of the shotgun past the ant's mouthparts and into its throat and fired. The ant's head flew backward and out of the doors. The doors closed and Burke turned to the airlock doors. He paused when he noticed the pool of reddish-yellow liquid on the floor. He studied the mess and found a partially melted nametag.

The only word Burke could make out on the tag was "Eric."

54.

David Braxton entered the trophy room of his home and walked to the bar. He poured himself a cognac and took a cigar from the humidor. He lit the cigar, removed his suit jacket, and fell into his favorite overstuffed leather chair. He took a drink, puffed his cigar, and gazed upward at his walls of memories. It had been a tiring week and he was spent. He sat enjoying his drink and his smoke for several minutes until the tranquility was broken by the ringing of his cell phone.

He instinctively reached for his inner jacket pocket then quickly realized he was no longer wearing his jacket. He cursed the call and stood and made his way back over to the bar where his jacket lay draped over a bar chair. He reached into his jacket, retrieved the phone, and held it to his ear.

"Hello."

There was no answer.

He dropped the cell phone in his pants pocket and turned to return to his chair.

He barely registered Burke before his right cross knocked him into unconsciousness.

55.

David awoke to a splitting headache and blinding sunlight.

He understood that he was lying down and he tried to stand but was unable. He looked to his right to see his outstretched arm tied to a stake in the ground. He spun his head around to see that his left arm was also tied to a stake. He pulled his legs and surmised that they too were tied to some kind of stake or pole. He struggled for a moment then felt warmth slide over his chest and thighs.

He was covered in some sort of liquid.

Some kind of thick liquid.

He continued struggling, trying with all his might to free himself.

He called out but heard nothing in return until a heavy weight fell to his side.

He jerked his head to his right to see what looked to be a mummy of some kind.

The sky above him darkened and he looked up to see Burke standing over him.

"That's what's left of your wife," Burke calmly announced. "That cribellate orb weaver wrapped her up good."

David shot his eyes back to the mummy. He suddenly understood where he was and suddenly had an idea of what was going on.

"Burke...let me go," David commanded. "Let me go this instant..."

"No," Burke said, smiling.

"What have you done to me?" David thrashed about, trying hopelessly to free himself.

"Ya know the old promise of coating your enemy in honey and staking them to an ant mound? Well, this is my take on that."

David's mind raced in utter panic. He thrashed and pulled, flailed and jerked to get free to no avail.

"Not that I really care," Burke said, changing direction. "It honestly doesn't matter to me, but why? Was it about love? Betrayal? Money? What? What would possess you to unleash this kind of pain on someone you shared your life with?"

"Money?!" David exclaimed. "You said money. You said money. How much do you want? You know I can pay you…"

"Yes. You have a lot of money. The kind of money that allows you to have things taken care of. Who took care of this for you?"

"Maria!" David blurted out in sheer panic. "Maria Flores. She works for me. This was her idea. I told her under no circumstances was she—"

"Maria Flores?"

"Yes! Maria Flores…"

"Okay." Burke nodded. "I'll pay her a visit next."

Burke turned and began walking away.

David called after him.

"Come back! Where are you going? Where are you…?"

Burke returned to his hovering position.

"Told you," Burke answered. "I'm gonna go pay Maria a visit…"

"I told you it was her! I didn't have anything to do with this. Let me go and I'll help you…"

"I don't need your help," Burke assured David. "I can take care of her all on my own…"

"Let me go and I can—"

"I gotta go." Burke smiled and pointed to the distance. "Ants are coming. And they ain't the kind you can step on or just flip aside."

Burke left and David struggled in panic to free himself. He screamed for Burke to return, cursed him, then wished him a horrible death. David was so busy screaming and thrashing about that he didn't hear the fire ants stampeding toward him.

He was only aware of them when one crouched over his face and opened its mandibles with a terrifying hiss.

THE END

ABOUT THE AUTHOR

"If you mixed Ernest Hemingway, Robert Ruark, Hunter S. Thompson, and four shots of tequila in a blender, a 'Gayne Young' is what you'd call the drink!" – Author Doug Howlett

Gayne C. Young is the former Editor-in-Chief of North American Hunter and North American Fisherman - both part of CBS Sports -and a columnist for and feature contributor to Sporting Classics magazine. His work has appeared in magazines such as Outdoor Life, Petersen's Hunting, Texas Sporting Journal, Sports Afield, Gray's Sporting Journal, Under Wild Skies, Hunter's Horn, Spearfishing, and many others. He is the author of Teddy Roosevelt: Sasquatch Hunter, Vikings: The Bigfoot Saga, Bigfoot, The Boggy Creek Narratives, And Monkeys Threw Crap At Me: Adventures In Hunting, Fishing, And Writing, and numerous other titles. His screenplay, Eaters Of Men was optioned in 2010 by the Academy Award winning production company of Kopelson Entertainment.

In January 2011, Gayne C. Young became the first American outdoor writer to interview Russian Prime Minister, and former Russian President, Vladimir Putin.

You can reach Gayne through the following
Email: gayne@gaynecyoung.com
Facebook Page: Gayne C. Young – Outdoor Writer
Facebook Personal: Gayne C. Young
Instagram: gayneyoung
Amazon Author Page: Gayne C. Young Author
Severed Press Author Page:
Webpage: Gayne C. Young

CHECK OUT OTHER GREAT HORROR NOVELS

DEATH CRAWLERS
by Gerry Griffiths

Worldwide, there are thought to be 8,000 species of centipede, of which, only 3,000 have been scientifically recorded. The venom of Scolopendra gigantea—the largest of the arthropod genus found in the Amazon rainforest—is so potent that it is fatal to small animals and toxic to humans. But when a cargo plane departs the Amazon region and crashes inside a national park in the United States, much larger and deadlier creatures escape the wreckage to roam wild, reproducing at an astounding rate. Entomologist, Frank Travis solicits small town sheriff Wanda Rafferty's help and together they investigate the crash site. But as a rash of gruesome deaths befalls the townsfolk of Prospect, Frank and Wanda will soon discover how vicious and cunning these new breed of predators can be. Meanwhile, Jake and Nora Carver, and another backpacking couple, are venturing up into the mountainous terrain of the park. If only they knew their fun-filled weekend is about to become a living nightmare.

THE PULLER
by Michael Hodges

Matt Kearns has two choices: fight or hide. The creature in the orchard took the rest. Three days ago, he arrived at his favorite place in the world, a remote shack in Michigan's Upper Peninsula. The plan was to mourn his father's death and figure out his life. Now he's fighting for it. An invisible creature has him trapped. Every time Matt tries to flee, he's dragged backwards by an unseen force. Alone and with no hope of rescue, Matt must escape the Puller's reach. But how do you free yourself from something you cannot see?

CHECK OUT OTHER GREAT
HORROR NOVELS

BLACK FRIDAY
by Michael Hodges

Jared the kleptomaniac, Onike the unemployed IT guy, Patricia the shopaholic, and Jeff the meth dealer are trapped inside a Chicago supermall on Black Friday. Bridgefield Mall empties during a fire alarm, and most of the shoppers drive off into a strange mist surrounding the mall parking lot. They never return. Onike and his group try calling friends and family, but their smart phones won't work, not even Twitter. As the mist creeps closer, the mall lights flicker and surge. Bulbs shatter and spray glass into the air. Unsettling noises are heard from within the mist, as the meth dealer becomes unhinged and hunts the group within the mall. Cornered by the mist, and hunted from within, Onike and the survivors must fight for their lives while solving the mystery of what happened to Bridgefield Mall. Sometimes, a good sale just isn't worth it.

GRIMWEAVE
by Tim Curran

In the deepest, darkest jungles of Indochina, an ancient evil is waiting in a forgotten, primeval valley. It is patient, monstrous, and bloodthirsty. Perfectly adapted to its hot, steaming environment, it strikes silent and stealthy. Its chosen prey: human. Now Michael Spiers, a Marine sniper, the only survivor of a previous encounter with the beast, is going after it again. Against his better judgement, he is made part of a Marine Force Recon team that will hunt it down and destroy it.

The hunters are about to become the hunted.

CHECK OUT OTHER GREAT HORROR NOVELS

MONSTROSITY
by Tim Curran

The Food. It seeped from the ground, a living, gushing, teratogenic nightmare. It contaminated anything that ate it, causing nature to run wild with horrible mutations, creating massive monstrosities that roam the land destroying towns and cities, feeding on livestock and human beings and one another. Now Frank Bowman, an ordinary farmer with no military skills, must get his children to safety. And that will mean a trip through the contaminated zone of monsters, madmen, and The Food itself. Only a fool would attempt it. Or a man with a mission.

THE SQUIRMING
by Jack Hamlyn

You are their hosts.

You are their food.

The parasites came out of nowhere, squirming horrors that enslaved the human race. They turned the population into mindless pack animals, psychotic cannibalistic hordes whose only purpose was to feed them.

Now with the human race teetering at the edge of extinction, extermination teams are fighting back, killing off the parasites and their voracious hosts. Taking them out one by one in violent, bloody encounters.

The future of mankind is at stake.

And time is running out.

www.ingramcontent.com/pod-product-compliance
Lightning Source LLC
Chambersburg PA
CBHW051958170626
46808CB00007B/2682